SHOUTYKID [...] ...k... If you like *Diary of a Wimpy [...]* or *Tom Gates* you will like this book... it's really funny and it made me laugh.
Isaac, age 8

Totally awesome... the trials of Harry *Riddles*'s life are laugh-out-loud funny. I could not stop laughing. Go out and grab a copy, you won't be disappointed.
Leia, age 10

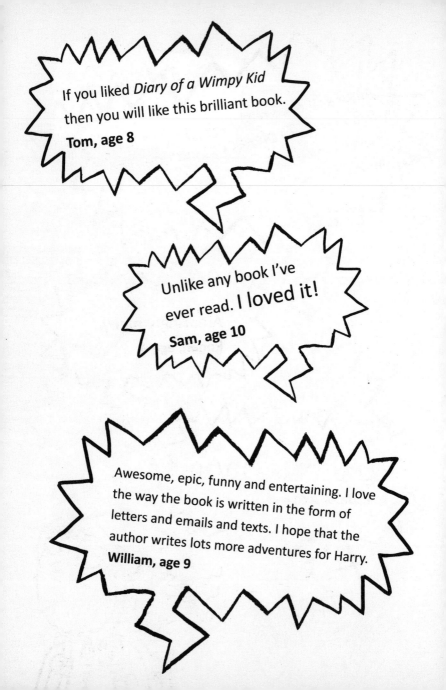

By the same author:

Shoutykid – *How Harry Riddles Made a Mega-amazing Zombie Movie*

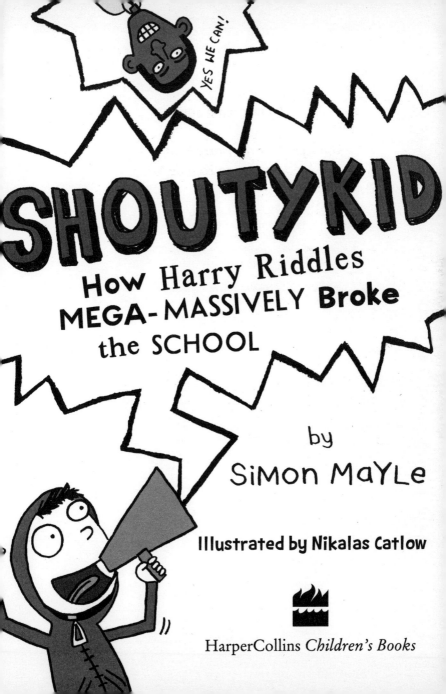

YES WE CAN!

SHOUTYKID

How Harry Riddles
MEGA-MASSIVELY Broke
the SCHOOL

by
SiMON MaYLe

Illustrated by Nikalas Catlow

HarperCollins *Children's Books*

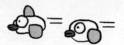

First published in Great Britain by HarperCollins *Children's Books* 2015
HarperCollins *Children's Books* is a division of HarperCollins*Publishers* Ltd,
HarperCollins *Publishers*
1 London Bridge Street
London SE1 9GF

The HarperCollins *Children's Books* website address is
www.harpercollins.co.uk

1

SHOUTYKID – HOW HARRY RIDDLES MEGA-MASSIVELY BROKE
THE SCHOOL
Text copyright © Simon Mayle 2015
Illustrations © Nikalas Catlow 2015

Simon Mayle and Nikalas Catlow assert the moral right to be
identified as the author and illustrator of this work.

ISBN 978-0-00-753189-9

Printed and bound in England by
Clays Ltd, St Ives plc

This book is for three very special young ladies:

Fauve, Ezeld and Olivia – with much love from your godfather xxx

CHAPTER ONE
DISNEYLAND

From Harry Riddles **to** Charley Riddles
Subject: Disneyland
28 December 20:05 GMT

Dear Cuz –

Thanks for sending me all those pictures of
you and everybody having such a great time at
Disneyland without us. Maybe next time you go,
we can ALL go. Then we can ALL ride the Pirates
of the Caribbean together, cos that ride looks like
LOTS of fun.

I know my dad's told your dad he's got some problems getting a visa to visit America, but don't worry cos I'm gonna mail your President and get him to straighten this out for us cos there's **NO WAY** we're gonna miss your high school graduation!

BTW – when I showed the photos of you guys to my mum, she started crying. I guess she really wants to get on that ride too. OK. That's all.

Good luck and have fun.

And GBTM soon.

Yr cousin,

Harry

HIS ROYAL HARRINESS

Tresinkum Farm
Cornwall PL36 0BH
28th December

The President
The White House
1600 Pennsylvania Avenue NW
Washington, DC 20500

Dear Mr President, hi there,

I don't know if anybody has talked to you about this yet, but my dad's having A LOT OF PROBLEMS getting a visa to visit your country. Can you sort this out so we can come and visit? Great! Thanks a lot!

BTW – if you need to know who I am, ask David

Cameron. He's our Prime Minister. He knows me, cos last year I wrote to him to see if he wanted to rent our house for the summer. He didn't, but he wrote back, so he can DEFINITELY vouch for me, OK?

Good luck and have fun.

Harry Riddles
Email: harryriddles1@gmail.com

PS sorry for getting you to sign for this, but we REALLY need that visa.

From Harry **to** Charley
29 December 10:08 GMT

Dear Cuz –

I've just mailed your President and if that guy's as quick to get back to me as our Prime Minister, my guess is we'll get that visa in, like, two weeks, then we can all relax. Unless there are any more family disasters.

BTW – how come you're never online any more? What's going on?

Harry

Cuz? U there? Wanna play some *World of Zombies*?
Harry

Squid – I'm here, but it's New Year's Eve so I'm NOT gonna be sitting in my room playing *World of Zombies* – not even with YOU!! Got it? Good. See ya!
Charley

Why not? You scared I'm gonna get pwnage over you?

From Charley **to** Harry
Subject: New Year's Eve
31 December 12:45 PST

Smurf –

I'm not scared, but, unlike you, I have a life
AWAY from a screen. And tonight is New Year's
Eve, which means I'm gonna go out with my
girlfriend and we're gonna PARTY – which is
what you should be doing with YOUR
GIRLFRIEND on New Year's Eve. Not spending
the night in front of a screen shooting stupid
zombies like some little weirdo freak.

Happy New Year!

Charley

From Harry **to** Charley
Subject: Little weirdo freaks
31 December 21:01 GMT

Dear Cuz –

Firstly, playing *World of Zombies* on my own
does not make me some little weirdo freak, but
it will make me a MASTER OF GRAND MASTERS
if I PRACTISE – which, BTW, would be totally
INCREDIBLE. But that means I have to practise
A LOT!

As for the girlfriend thing? I would definitely
be with my girlfriend if I HAD a girlfriend, but I
don't, cos the only girl I really like is Jessica. And
she's gone skiing with her family, so I won't see
her till I go back to my school. But when I do see

her, I'm gonna tell her how much I like her. Then I'm gonna ask her if we can go out. And then I'll have a girlfriend just like you, which would be pretty AWESOME! So that's my plan for this term. Become a Master of Grand Masters and start going out with Jessica.

So good luck and have fun. And have a HAPPY NEW YEAR!!!!

Harry

BTW – my mum and dad told me and my sister they have some REALLY exciting news to share with us. I'm just hoping it's that new Xbox One, cos that's LONG overdue in this house!!!

From The White House **to** Harry Riddles
Subject: Request from David Cameron's friend
03 January 10:15 EST

Dear Friend,

Thank you for your message. On behalf of
President Obama, we appreciate hearing from you.
The President has promised the most transparent
administration in history, and we are committed to
listening to and responding to you.

Sincerely,

The Presidential Correspondence Team

From Harry **to** The White House
03 January 15:17 GMT

Dear The Presidential Correspondence Team,

Thanks a lot for getting back to me. And congratulations for being so transparent (whatever THAT means), but what's going on with my dad's visa?

Please tell the President I'm keeping my fingers crossed he's gonna fix this for us ASAP. And BTW – I think it means a LOT to my mum, cos last night at dinner we started talking about NOT making it out to California and she started CRYING again. Even when my sister pointed out that we've got MONTHS before my cousin Charley graduates, she just kept saying how sad it would be if we couldn't all go see him get his high school diploma, cos our dad never got one. So at least SOMEONE in this family is going to finish high school!!! So this is like a very BIG DEAL for her. Can you guys make her happy? I don't like it when she gets upset. Thanks a lot!

Good luck and have fun.

Harry Riddles

BTW – Does the President play *World of Zombies*? If he does and he needs some expert tuition, I'm willing to make a trade of a visa for one, or possibly TWO elite gaming prestiges – unless he really sucks.

04 January 18:42 GMT

 Kid Zombie: OMG – look who it is! It's my Most Valued Player cuz! Where you been, stranger?

 MVP Guy: Oh you know, off somewhere having a life. But don't worry, the MVP is back. You have a good New Year up in your room blasting yr little zombies?

 Kid Zombie: Not really.

MVP Guy: Why not?

 Kid Zombie: Cos my mum and dad dropped a BOMB on this house!

 MVP Guy: Oh yeah? What happened?

 Kid Zombie: You know I told you they had this really exciting news they wanted to share?

 MVP Guy: Sure.

 Kid Zombie: OK, so I'm thinking, GREAT! Here we go! The big news is gonna be we're getting that new Xbox One!!!

MVP Guy: That's the bomb?

 Kid Zombie: No. The bomb is when my mum tells me and Charlotte that she's PREGNANT!!!

 MVP Guy: At their age?

 Kid Zombie: That's what my sister said.

 MVP Guy: She said that?

 Kid Zombie: No - what she said was, it was, like, the WORST NEWS SHE'S EVER HEARD and they were CRAZY having a baby, cos they were, like, so ANCIENT!!! Plus – where was IT going to sleep? We don't have spare bedrooms!

 MVP Guy: Lol, man. What did they say?

 Kid Zombie: They didn't say anything, cos Charlotte didn't let 'em. She said having another kid was THE most selfish thing they could have done to us, and how was she supposed to concentrate on her 'career' as a famous pop star with a screaming baby in the house? So I said, "What career? You haven't even had your first gig yet. You probably suck!"

 MVP Guy: NICE. So then what happens?

Kid Zombie: So then, like, my dad has to hold her back cos she wants to hit me! But come on! Where did she get that DUMB idea from? Actually, I know where she got it from. Spencer. That kid will say anything to get her off his back. Even something as crazy as her becoming a POP STAR!

MVP Guy: What did your mum say?

Kid Zombie: She got upset. Then she said she didn't get pregnant on PURPOSE, she got pregnant by ACCIDENT. But my sister said having a car crash is an accident. Breaking an arm is an accident. But having a baby? That's not an accident, that's a DECLARATION OF WAR!!!

MVP Guy: Lol.

Kid Zombie: But you know what was really funny? My dad says, "We're not having one baby, Charlotte! We're having TWINS!!!" Well, that sent my sister into ORBIT! (Which, BTW, was pretty hilarious - until she said, "I don't know what you're laughing about! They're going to be in YOUR room, not MINE, you little idiot!!! HA!!!")

MVP Guy: So what are you gonna do?

Kid Zombie: Do what I always do! FIX IT!!!

CHAPTER THREE

THE WINDSORS

HIS ROYAL HARRINESS

Tresinkum Farm
Cornwall PL36 0BH
4th January

The Duke and Duchess of Cambridge
Clarence House
London SW1A 1BA

Dear the Duke and Duchess of Cambridge, hi there,

My name is Harry and last year I wrote to your nan and asked her if we could come and live with you guys up at Buckingham Palace, cos my dad had lost his job and basically we were pretty broke.

Your nan was really cool and she wrote back and said how sorry she was to hear about our news, but we couldn't move in with her up at the palace – which was fine, cos my dad got a job down at SuperSave, so we didn't lose our home and everything worked out OK again. THANK GOD!

Until TWO days ago. Then my mum tells me and my sister that she was gonna have some TWINS, which means ONE of us is gonna have to give up our ROOM!!! And THIS is where you guys come in. Do you need an au pair?

Last week, my sister told my mum that she might like a job if she was working for a nice family. So I thought of you. Plus (and this is a BIG plus), Kensington Palace is A LONG WAY from Cornwall – so my sister will NOT be able to come home every w/e (which would be GREAT cos then I wouldn't have to hide all my stuff when she's in a bad mood, which is basically 24/7).

Plus, my sister is REALLY GOOD with kids (as long as they are not me). And she wants to be a pop star, which means your son will get a great musical education (as long as he likes Beyoncé). And, if you guys need a break, she and Spencer can take him camping at Glastonbury (where they are going this summer), which he will LOVE, cos that place is ALWAYS MUDDY!!

Please get back to me soon and tell me when you want her to start (but can it be before the twins are born on 17th May?). Great! Thanks a lot!

Good luck and have fun.

Harry Riddles

From Harry **to** Charley
05 January 09:22 GMT

Dear Cuz –

Keep your fingers crossed the Windsors need an
au pair. Otherwise, it's Plan B.

Harry

———————————————————

From Charley **to** Harry
05 January 08:13 PST

What's Plan B?

HIS ROYAL HARRINESS

Tresinkum Farm
Cornwall PL36 0BH
5th January

Sir Philip Green
Arcadia Group
Colegrave House
70 Berners Street
London W1T 3NL

Dear Sir Philip Green, owner of Topshop, my
sister's favourite fashion store, hi there,

Can you give my sister a job at your flagship
store in central London so she can come and

live up in London? On your website it says you are looking for people who have pride, passion and energy, but mostly love Topshop. Well, my sister LOVES Topshop. She says your shop is the most brilliant shop in the whole world and she wants everything you make, so you could not find a bigger fan, ANYWHERE. In fact, the only time she's EVER in a good mood is when she knows she's going to Topshop in Plymouth for the day.

On your website it also says you want to know if any person who wants to work for you would be great at delivering the ULTIMATE SHOPPING EXPERIENCE! I'd say most definitely, cos my sister knows where everything is, how much everything costs, when the shop shuts, when the sales are, and where you can get the bus home, which is pretty much all you need to know, right?

My only worry is the team player thing. Until last term, my sister WAS captain of the school hockey team, but she got demoted for biting this girl from the local convent school. But this girl kept trying to break my sister's legs with her hockey stick, so my sister was just sticking up for herself – which I think is kind of OK. So, as long as your customers DON'T have hockey sticks and DON'T want to break my sister's legs, she won't bite anybody (fingers crossed).

Please get back to me soon and let me know when she can start, so I can help her pack her stuff. OK? Great! Thanks a lot!

Good luck and have fun.

Harry Riddles

From Harry **to** Charley
05 January 17:18 GMT

Cuz –

I think the Charlotte problem is now SOLVED.
But I talked to my friend Walnut about the twins
and he said he couldn't BELIEVE how lucky I was.
He said if these twins grow up like me, we will
be the ULTIMATE FIGHTING FORCE on *World of
Zombies*!

From Charley **to** Harry
05 January 09:21 PST

Yeah, but what happens if they are SISTERS
and not BROTHERS? What if you get two more
Charlottes? Then what are you going to do?

From Harry **to** Charley
05 January 17:25 GMT

Cuz –

Firstly, they are not going to be like my sister, cos nobody could POSSIBLY be as evil as her. So probably they will be like my mum – in which case they will be really nice and really sweet and be the sisters I wish Charlotte was. Not the High Priestess of Evil that Charlotte really is.

U wanna go see a movie when
I get back from town? Just you
and me?
Dad

Can I bring Walnut?
Harry

Maybe better just you and me.

From Harry **to** Charley
05 January 21:45 GMT

Dear Cuz –

Tonight my dad took me to the movies (you know that cinema that really STINKS? We went there and guess what? It STILL stinks!). Then we went out and had a pizza and he asked me how I felt about having some more family members on the way. I told him I like our family the way it is. Plus, I like being the youngest. So then my dad said, "Yeah, but won't it be great when we can all go surfing together? Or skateboarding?!" So I said, "Or when I teach 'em how to play *WORLD OF ZOMBIES*!!!"

Well, my dad didn't like that idea AT ALL. He said it's bad enough having one gamer in the family. He doesn't want either of them growing up like me. I said, "What's wrong with me?" He said, "You know what I mean, Harry. Spending all day staring at a computer screen – that's not a good way for a kid to grow up." I said, "How would I know? You never allow me to game all day." He said, "I just wish you'd give other stuff a chance."

So then he said that, from the beginning of term tomorrow, him and my mum were going to cut back on the hours I'm allowed to go online, and then maybe I'll be more like Walnut and spend more time playing sport. I said, "I don't want to be more like Walnut. Walnut is best at being Walnut and I'm best at being Harry. Why change things?"

Then I got upset and Dad said it's no big deal, but have a think about it, cos if I spent half the time I spend gaming doing something else, maybe I'd be really good at doing that something else. After that, I didn't want to talk to him cos he made me feel rubbish. Maybe he thinks these twins are going to turn out to be the kids he wishes I was. I wish they weren't coming.

Harry

_____

From Charley **to** Harry
05 January 13:55 PST

Cuz -

Your pops just wants you to get out of the house and start playing MORE sport and LESS *World of Zombies*. That's all.

BTW – You back to school tomorrow? How's yr girl?

CHAPTER FOUR

HELMET

World of ZOMBIES
Community Forum

06 January 19:02 GMT

Kid Zombie: Walnut - you on?

Goofykinggrommet: Wassup, Harry? How's school?

Kid Zombie: OK, I guess. Weird, maybe. I don't know.

Goofykinggrommet: I thought you were looking forward to going back? Seeing what's-her-name?

Kid Zombie: Jessica?

 Goofykinggrommet: Yeah. Jessica.

 Kid Zombie: Well, I was.

 Goofykinggrommet: And what happened?

 Kid Zombie: I don't know.

 Goofykinggrommet: Whaddya mean?

Kid Zombie: I mean, like, I get back to my school and I really can't wait to see her again. I mean, like, REALLY can't wait. But when I finally get to talk to her, she starts telling me how she's just had the BEST skiing holiday of her LIFE, and wishes it had NEVER ended. So I asked her why, but already I could tell something pretty bad was coming. So then she tells me about this kid called Helmet, who is really good at skiing, and is a really great sportsman, and how he took her on these really great trails that nobody knew about, and what a brilliant, brilliant time they had hanging out together.

Goofykinggrommet: Well, that kinda sucks.

Kid Zombie: That's what I thought.

Goofykinggrommet: So then what happens?

 Kid Zombie: So then I asked her how old this Helmet kid was and she said he was, like, twelve or thirteen. A LOT older than me. So I said that's a pretty unusual name, Helmet. And she said, it's Helmut, Harry. Not Helmet. And he lives in a castle and comes from some place that sounds like Hamburgers. And maybe next year, if I came skiing, I could meet him and we could all go skiing together and then I'd see what a great, great kid he is.

I thought, you gotta be kidding me, right? I mean, I've never skied in my life and why would I want to meet this Helmet-from-Hamburgers kid? But then I thought maybe if I DID learn how to ski, I could spend the Christmas holidays with her, cos I never see her much at my school.

Goofykinggrommet: You know what you should do? Snowboarding. Snowboarding is like the COOLEST thing I ever did. I went with my school. We took this coach all the way to Austria and had a Wally of the Week competition, which was really good FUN, BTW!!

Kid Zombie: Yeah, well, if you had Ed Bigstock on your coach, you wouldn't need to have a Wally of the Week competition, cos that kid is The King of the Wallies of the Week, EVERY week. You know what he said to me when he saw me speaking to Jessica? He said how HILARIOUS he thinks it would be if I went skiing with the SCHOOL! So I asked him why and he said because I suck at sport, cos I'm just a STUPID GAMER!

Goofykinggrommet: Yeah – but you kick ass at gaming, Harry!

Kid Zombie: Jessica is not impressed with gamers. Nor is my dad. Or my mum. You know what happens every time my mum gets a kick in the stomach from one of the twins? My dad says these kids are gonna play for England! I think he means it too. Like he wants them to grow up and be FOOTBALLERS!!!

 Goofykinggrommet: My dad's the same. He hates gamers. Gotta go – mum's calling.

From Harry **to** Charley
09 January 18:42 GMT

Dear Cuz –

We've got football trials next week and I'm starting to wonder if I should do it to show my dad I'm not just a stupid gamer kid. My only problem is I never play football. What do you think I should do?

Harry

From Charley **to** Harry
09 January 18:05 PST

Do you suck at all sport?

From Harry **to** Charley
10 January 08:04 GMT

I'd say I was probably the WORST athlete in my school, if it weren't for Bulmer. Bulmer is the only kid who refuses to run anywhere, cos he has asthma and says it's bad for his health. Either he walks, or he doesn't move. Every school should have a Bulmer. The kid's a legend and makes me look like Usain Bolt.

Harry

From Charley **to** Harry
10 January 19:05 PST

Squid –

Give it a shot. What's the worst thing that could happen? You don't make the team. Big deal. At least you tried and made everybody happy. Let me know what happens.

Charley

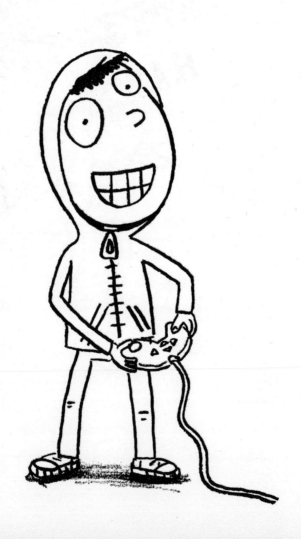

CHAPTER FIVE
H.A.W.G.

Harry to Charley

Bad news. The Windsors don't want the psycho.
Harry

What about the job in the shop?
Charley

From Harry **to** Charley
13 January 21:21 GMT

I dunno. He hasn't written back. But you know what the GOOD news is? I talked to my headmaster and asked him if I could set up my own computer club and he said that was a GREAT IDEA, cos computer science is a really important subject and he wants more kids to learn how to write COMPUTER CODE, cos coding is THE language of the FUTURE. I didn't tell him my club was NOT about learning how to write the language of the future, but learning how to KICK ASS at video games when your mum and dad want to cut down on your GAME TIME.

Anyway, now I have my own club, which, BTW, is called H.A.W.G. (Harry's Awesome World of Games) and it's gonna be totally GREAT! So if you want to join, let me know, then I can send you a password.

Gotta go. Football trial tomorrow!

Yr cuz,

Harry

What happened at
the football trial?
Charley

OMG incredible.
Harry

Whaddya mean?

I'm in the team!!!

How u manage that?

From Harry **to** Charley
14 January 17:58 GMT

Well, basically our school SUCKS at football, so getting in the team is not what you might call hard. In fact, I figured all I had to do was show up, put my hand in the air, and I was in.

That was it?
Charley

No. Bit more than that.
Harry

You had to kick a
ball? What a surprise!

I know – that's kinda what I
thought. Anyway, I nearly didn't
bother, cos things got pretty
scary, PDQ.

How come?

72

From Harry **to** Charley
14 January 20:16 GMT

That idiot, Bigstock. When I got down there,
that kid was already smashing balls into the net,
showing everybody how great he was at football.
But as soon as he sees me, he starts shouting,
"Oh my God – look who it is! The little geek!!!
What the hell are you doing down here, Harry?
Computer room's thataway! HA HA HA!!!"

Which was kind of what I was expecting him to
say. But the size thing? That got my goat, cos
he always has to point out that I'm the smallest

kid in my class (and the youngest), but I never point out that he's just a FREAK of NATURE and a dimwit, cos I know what would happen if I did.

Anyway, I'm standing there on the pitch and Mr Phillips is getting everybody who turned up to take a penalty to see if anybody can get it anywhere near the net (which I thought UNLIKELY). And that's when I see Jessica playing hockey on the next pitch. So she waves to me.

And I wave back. And then I watch Bulmer and Oscar da Silva step up and take their penalties. And guess what? They both get the ball in the back of the net!! Which kinda made me feel not so great. So I'm just thinking about bailing, when I get a text from my dad asking me if I thought the name Ronaldo, or Ronalda, was a cool name for one of the twins (after the footballer). Well, that did it. I wasn't gonna quit. Who needs a Ronaldo or Ronalda Riddles in the family when we have ME?

From Charley **to** Harry
14 January 18:22 PST

See – now you're making sense. Get competitive and get in their FACE. So what happened?

OK – so, like, then I walk out on the pitch and I hear Bigstock yell to Jessica to come over quick, cos I was about to make Mount Joseph history and kick a real football! So Jessica comes over with some of her friends and now I really am getting a little panicky, cos the stakes have gone up BIG TIME and my confidence has pretty much DISAPPEARED. Anyway, what do I know about taking penalties? The only penalty I take is when I bail from a league game in *WoZ* and they strip me 400 points.

So I'm waiting by the ball and everything gets, like, a million times worse when the headmaster rolls in to check out what's going on. So now we have this big crowd on the touchline, ALL waiting to watch me kick a stupid penalty.

Well, now I'm definitely NOT wanting to do this. I'm thinking I might even be starting to have a PANIC ATTACK, cos my breathing's getting difficult and I'm feeling a bit dizzy. So I start my walk back from the ball. And I keep on WALKING all the way to the halfway line, where there's this thick blanket of FOG that's just rolled on to the pitch. I figure if I can just get INTO that fog and DISAPPEAR, Jessica and the headmaster will think I've gone off to take an early bath and not had a major meltdown.

But just before I get there, I hear Mr Phillips shout, "Harry? Where you going? Net's this way! Let's go!"

So now I really am feeling ILL. And THAT'S when I suddenly remembered sitting with my dad in front of the TV, watching Tuesday Night Football. My dad was telling Wayne Rooney how he should take a penalty. "Kick the ball as hard as you can, Wayne!" he said. "Take his head off. Works every time!"

So that's what I figured I'd TRY and do. Kick the ball as HARD as possible. Hopefully, Bulmer will duck. Hopefully, I won't take his head off. And hopefully the ball will go straight in the back of the net. Hopefully. But probably not, knowing my luck.

So I start my run. But it's a LONG way from the halfway circle down to the penalty box. And by the time I get down near the goal, I'm out of breath, my legs are like jelly, and I know I'm definitely gonna miss this penalty. So I start to swing my leg back and that's when I hear Bigstock shout, "YOUR BABY SISTERS COULD DO THIS BETTER, YOU LITTLE LOSER!!!"

And those simple words from that moron was all the motivation I needed. I kicked that ball as hard as I could and it BLASTED straight into the top right hand corner of the net, saving Bulmer the opportunity of even having to THINK about moving across to stop it.

So I scored an amazing goal. Even the headmaster came up to me after and said how SURPRISED and IMPRESSED he was by my cool head under pressure and my great penalty-taking skills. And that was my excellent football trial.

Now I'm in the team and they think I'm some kind of penalty expert, which is pretty crazy, but, like I said, we suck, so there's not much talent to choose from. But who cares? When my dad gets home I'm gonna tell him Harry Riddles made it to the Colts XI, and he better be really PLEASED, cos this is gonna wreck my Wednesdays, which, BTW, is like the ONLY day I'm allowed to game after school.

But I guess I had to do something, cos me and my dad don't hang out much any more cos he's been away a lot and when he Skypes, it's ALWAYS when I'm gaming and he gets kinda upset if I'm on a mission and I don't want to talk to him.

Harry

From Charley **to** Harry
15 January 08:02 PST

Trust me – it's worth losing yr Wednesdays.

CHAPTER SIX
PULL MY FINGER

World of ZOMBIES
COMMUNITY FORUM

16 January 19:34 GMT

Kid Zombie: Walnut? You online?

Goofykinggrommet: Hey Harry. Wassup?

Kid Zombie: Twins. That's all anybody talks about round here. U know I got on the football team, right?

Goofykinggrommet: Yeah. That's GREAT - I'll bet yr dad loved that!

 Kid Zombie: Kind of.

 Goofykinggrommet: Whaddya mean?

 Kid Zombie: I mean I think he was pleased, but I don't think he could understand HOW I got on the team, cos he knows I never play football. How r u?

 Goofykinggrommet: Good.

 Kid Zombie: We're going bowling at the w/e. Wanna come?

Goofykinggrommet: I think there's, like, this BBQ thing down at Area 51 skate park and my dad wants me to go to that. Gonna be mega. Why don't you come?

 Kid Zombie: I don't skateboard.

 Goofykinggrommet: Maybe it's time you learnt.

 Kid Zombie: U sound like my dad. U know how tough it is to get online in my house? IMPOSSIBLE!! I came home from school yesterday and my mum says, "Why don't you give gaming a night off, Harry? Sort out your toy chest instead?" And before I can say anything, she takes away my phone. So I think, OK, you want to play tough, I can do that. So I tell my mum, "You know what? That's a really GREAT idea! I'll go to my room and sort out my toys and then, the stuff I don't want, you can take to the charity shop!!" And my mum smiles and tells me what a good kid I am. But I don't tell her there's an old iPod in that toy chest that she's probably forgotten about. So I get up to my room and I dig around in the chest and I empty all my toys all over my bedroom floor and then my mum comes in and says, "Is this what you're looking for, Harry?" And she's holding up my old iPod!!! OMG, my mum is so SMART!!!

 Goofykinggrommet: Yeah, mine too. Calling me now for dinner – gotta go.

 Kid Zombie: Yup.

From Harry **to** Charley
18 January 11:14 GMT

Dear Cuz –

OMG – we got BAAAAAAAD news. Last night, we go bowling at the Leisure Centre, which could have been a great night, but just as we get there Spencer and my sister start having this fight over some surfer called Geoff, who kept staring at Charlotte and winking. So Charlotte goes over to talk to him and Spencer gets upset. So my mum sends ME over to get Charlotte and this kid says, "Pull my finger, Harry!" So I pull his finger and the kid farts, which was pretty dumb, but my sister laughed cos I guess she thought having a farting finger was pretty unusual.

Anyway, I get her back to where we're playing and basically my mum and her have this big fight. My mum tells my sister to be NICER to Spencer and more CONSIDERATE of his feelings, cos he's, like, part of our family.

Well, then it gets crazy, cos my sister yells at my mum that she's a HYPOCRITE and how can she criticise her for being inconsiderate of people's feelings, when my mum was so INCONSIDERATE of HER feelings when she got PREGNANT!

So then my mum gets upset and the next thing is she's holding her belly and telling my dad she's starting to feel funny and can we go home? Which was bad, but it got a whole lot WORSE in the car. My dad tells me, Charlotte and Spencer that we're definitely NOT going to make it out to America for your graduation. So I ask why and he says it will be TOO much travelling with the twins and blah, blah, blah, blah, blah. I didn't listen to the rest of it. But basically that's the news. We're not coming, cos of those stupid twins. So maybe my sister was right after all. Maybe it IS war between us and them!

Harry

CHAPTER SEVEN
THE BEAUTIFUL GAME

From Harry **to** Charley
20 January 16:01 GMT

Cuz –

Bigstock has done it to me again. I hate that kid.

From Charley **to** Harry
20 January 08:03 PST

What did he do this time?

From Harry **to** Charley
20 January 16:15 GMT

Basically, he turned up at my computer club cos
Bulmer and Oscar had told him how cool it was

to play games at school. But I didn't want that bully in my club, so I told him he couldn't join. He said, "Why not?" I said, "We have certain membership requirements that it's important to maintain." What I DIDN'T tell him was that we didn't let idiots in our club, cos I knew what would happen if I did.

Instead, I figured I'd nail him on the one thing I know where he REALLY sucks: General Core Gaming Skills. Bound to be poor, cos the kid always has a rugby ball in his hand. So I said, "Bigstock, you wanna join my club, there's an entrance test you have to pass. You fail, you don't get in. It has nothing to do with whether I think you're an idiot, or not. Deal?"

"DEAL, LOSER!!" he shouts at me. So I give him my phone and tell him, if he can get the bird through ten posts, he's in. Well, he couldn't even get that bird past TWO posts. Not even after three goes. So I said, "HA! You suck eggs, Ed! Give me the phone back, LOSER!"

From Charley **to** Harry
20 January 08:19 PST

U said that to Bigstock?

From Harry **to** Charley
20 January 16:32 GMT

I WISH I said that to Bigstock! What I actually said was, "Oh my gosh, you are SO unlucky, Ed. I am surprised a kid like you is so BAD at this game, when you are so GREAT at football and cricket and rugby and basically anything that involves a ball! But never mind! Can't win 'em all, can you?"

"Why not?" he shouts in my ear. "I normally do!"

Anyway, then the headmaster walks in with some new parents and he wants me to tell them a little bit about what we do in my computer club. But before I can say a word, Bigstock drops me in it and says, "Harry plays games, sir! That's all Harry does in here! Cos his dad doesn't like him doing it at home! Right, Harry?"

Well, judging by the look on my headmaster's face, I knew I needed to come up with something FAST, or he'd definitely close my club down. So I said, "That's right, Ed – we do PLAY GAMES here in the computer lab, but that's because it's RESEARCH for our school computing project, which is to MAKE OUR OWN COMPUTER GAME!!!!"

Well, as soon as I said THAT my headmaster started beaming from ear to ear, because this is EXACTLY the sort of stuff you're meant to be doing in a computer club if you want to get new parents to send their kids to your school.

So he says, "Great, Harry! We look forward to your first presentation!" I said, "What presentation?" And he said, "The presentation where you give a talk to the school, with a demonstration of your new game when it's finished!"

Then he tells me he wants to see it in, like, two weeks!!! And before I could argue, he was gone. So it's either I make a game, or he'll shut down my club. All because of Bigstock. Him and the twins are now at the top of my list of who-I-could-live-without-for-the-rest-of-my-LIFE!

Harry

U'll never make a game.
Charley

U said that about my movie, but
I made THAT, didn't I? HA!!!!!
Harry

Pups – got my first game on Wednesday. Wanna come watch? Harry

U'r in the team? Dad

I told you I was in the team. Don't u remember?

Oh yeah – sorry! I'll be there! Great news! Well done!

Dad... Game starts in 10. Where r u?

H – sorry. Have to go to doctor with Mum. Nothing serious. Dad xx

From Harry **to** Charley
22 January 18:14 GMT

Dear Cuz –

We had our first match today and guess where
I played? First reserve! Which basically meant
I was ball boy, which was pretty great until
Bigstock discovered that if he kicked the ball in
the lake, I had to fetch it. But I guess that's the
price I have to pay for not letting that idiot join
my computer club. Anyway, it was INCREDIBLE,
cos we only lost the game by three goals, so that
was a GREAT start for Mount Joseph's. If we keep
this up, we might even win a match! And when
we do, maybe my dad will be there to watch!!!

Harry

22 January 20:42 GMT

 Kid Zombie: Walnut? I need your help.

 Goofykinggrommet: Doing what?

 Kid Zombie: I need to make a video game to show my headmaster, or he's going to shut down my computer club.

Goofykinggrommet: How u going to do that?

 Kid Zombie: I dunno. But first I gotta figure out what game to make? U got any ideas?

 Goofykinggrommet: Zombies!!!

 Kid Zombie: OMG! GREAT IDEA!!! Maybe, like, in *Tetris* Zombies?

 Goofykinggrommet: Yeah, yeah – or, *Minecraft* Zombies?! Or, I don't know. What about *Super Mario* Zombies?!!

 Kid Zombie: But I'm thinking maybe it should be more like a phone game? Have you seen how hard it is to write computer code? It could take me YEARS! I've got, like, two weeks!

 Goofykinggrommet: So what are you going to do?

 Kid Zombie: Get help, I guess.

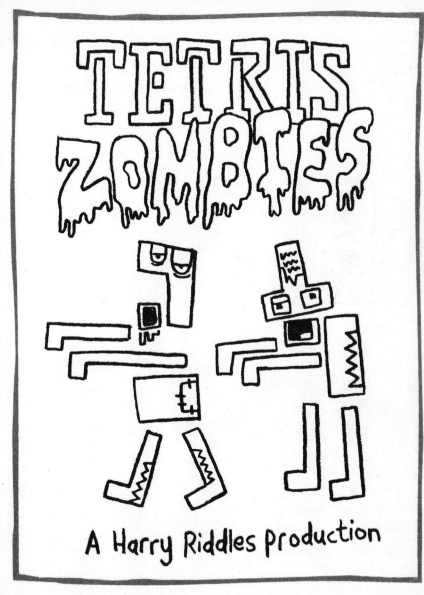

TETRIS ZOMBIES

A Harry Riddles production

From Harry **to** Activision Games
Subject: How to build cool games
23 January 18:05 GMT

Dear Activision Games, makers of *Call of Duty* and other cool games, hi there,

I told my headmaster I was making a game for my computer club, but I have NO idea how to build a game. When I talked to my mum, she said I should make a nice game like the one she always plays on her iPad – *Pet Rescue*. You know the one where you save a pet from falling down this stack of stuff?

So I thought maybe I could make a game called *Zombie Rescue*. So, instead of saving a pet when you move stuff around, you save a poor zombie. My question is: How do I make this in, like, two weeks and stick it on my phone?

GBTM soon.

Good luck and have fun.

Harry Riddles.

Squid – you finished
yr game?
Charley

From Harry **to** Charley
23 January 18:59 GMT

U kiddin'? But you know what the BEST news around here is? I'm *WORLD OF ZOMBIES* COMMUNITY MEMBER OF THE WEEK!!! Check out this link.

What started as a personal challenge to usurp the legendary IAMGOD's dominance in the World of Zombies *revealed a gamer of rare skill, cunning and smarts. From* World of Zombies, *to* World of Zombies 2 (Alien Nation), *Harry Riddles aka Kid Zombie has managed to achieve the extraordinary feat of a maximum of seven (that's right, gamers – SEVEN!) elite gaming prestiges for EACH game, which makes him ZOMBIE COMMUNITY MEMBER OF THE WEEK!!*

A FEW FACTS ABOUT THE KID AND HOW HE PWNS NUBS AND BEATS SCRUBS:

Gamer tag: Kid Zombie

Origin of gamer tag: It's what my sister calls me.

Current clan/Community: ZombieSniperUnit.

***World of Zombies* game(s) you are currently playing:** *World of Zombies*, *World of Zombies 2*.

Favorite map, game type and playlist: My favourite map is lost boys. My favorite game type is quick scope. And my favourite playlist is *WoZ* KWEP.

World of Zombies playing style: I like sniping with quick scope and doing whatever me and Walnut need to do to win BIG!!!!

Favourite *World of Zombies* character: Chewyerheadoff.

Anything else we should know? Yeah – your game totally rocks but I want to build my own phone game, so how do I do that? Please get back in touch with me at harryriddles1@gmail.com and tell me what I have to do. OK? Great! Thanks a lot!

Good luck and have fun.

Harry Riddles

From techsupport@worldofzombies.com
to harryriddlesl@gmail.com
24 January 09:32 GMT

Dear Harry –

As a valued friend and community member of
WoZ, I have been asked to assist you in your task of
building the next great *World of Zombies* storyline
for our FANTASTIC WORLD-CONQUERING
FRANCHISE. What did you have in mind?

techsupport@worldofzombies.com

———————————————

From Harry **to** techsupport@worldofzombies.com
24 January 19:10 GMT

Dear tech support –

I think you might have the wrong end of the

stick, cos I don't want to make a fantastic world-conquering franchise game for *World of Zombies* (no offence), cos that will take me, like, YEARS and I've only got, like, nine days. What I was thinking of was a phone game? Like you buy from the app store? Can you help me make that?

Kid Zombie

_____

From techsupport@worldofzombies.com
to harryriddles1@gmail.com
26 January 15:13 GMT

Hi Kid Zombie,

World of Zombies does not make phone games.

From Harry **to** techsupport@worldofzombies.com

26 January 20:12 GMT

Hi tech support –

OK. So who can help me?

Kid Zombie

From Guy Fox **to** Harry
Subject: Re: Building cool games...
27 January 18:04 GMT

Hi Kid Zombie –

Congratulations on being community zombie
member of the week!! Seven elite gaming
prestiges?? That's some impressive gaming! I
myself have only got six, so you must be one gr8
shooter! You said you were looking to build your
own phone game? I build phone games. That's
what I do in my command and control centre. So
if you want some help, let me know and I'll see
what I can do. What have you got in mind?

Guy Fox

From Harry **to** Guy Fox
27 January 19:28 GMT

Hi Guy Fox –

Thanks for writing back to me. What I want is
something like that flappy bird game. Can you
help me make one of them?

Kid Zombie

From Guy Fox **to** Harry
27 January 20:14 GMT

Kid Zombie –

I certainly can and I think that's a most
EXCELLENT idea!!

Guy Fox

From Harry **to** Guy Fox
27 January 21:02 GMT

Guy Fox –

OK. How do we do it?

Harry

_____

From Guy Fox **to** Harry
28 January 11:03 GMT

Kid Zombie –

Are you familiar with the re-skinning of games?
It's a really cool thing to do. I send you the code
for the game, then all you need to do is change
the graphics for the main characters in the game,

change your SFX, *et voilà* – you have your own new game that plays EXACTLY like the OLD game, but with NEW characters and NEW SFX and a NEW title. How do you like that idea?

Guy Fox

From Harry **to** Guy Fox
28 January 17:01 GMT

Guy Fox –

How do I like that idea? I LOVE THAT IDEA! That idea sounds like such a COOL idea!! Do you have the code for the bird game?

Kid Zombie

From Guy Fox **to** Harry
29 January 10:07 GMT

Kid Zombie –

Of course – but what kind of computer set-up
have you got? You'll need a network of computers,
like, I don't know – maybe the ones you have at
school? Only then will u be able to re-skin my
game to be the game you want!

Guy Fox

_____

From Harry **to** Guy Fox
29 January 17:51 GMT

Hi Guy Fox –

I could use my computers at school, cos I'm

in the computer club. But I don't know if they would let me, cos they don't want their network hacked by hackers.

Kid Zombie

From Guy Fox **to** Harry
29 January 18:15 GMT

Kid Zombie –

WHO wants to hack a stupid school computer network? That's ridiculous!

Guy Fox

From Harry **to** Guy Fox

29 January 18:53 GMT

I know. But they got rules.

From Guy Fox **to** Harry

29 January 18:56 GMT

Kid Zombie –

Rules are meant to be broken. R u with me on that?

From Harry **to** Guy Fox

29 January 18:58 GMT

Guy Fox –

Not sure I am. In fact, I'm not. OK? Sorry! Bye!

CHAPTER NINE

BEND IT LIKE BECKHAM

From Harry **to** Charley
30 January 18:18 GMT

Dear Cuz –

You know that kid, Helmet? He wrote a letter to Jessica and told her he was going to be taking a trial for some big German football team, which Jessica thought was, like, SO cool. Then the kid said he was thinking of coming over to visit. Jessica told me, if he came, he could come and look at the Colts and maybe give us some coaching tips, cos Mr Phillips is probably going to be leaving at the end of term, and he's more a rugby coach, anyway. I told her I don't think we need Helmet. We're doing just fine as it is. But she said Ed Bigstock had told her we hadn't got a chance in the South-West Schools' Cup because we don't know how to play as a team.

When I said to Bigstock, "If I find us a new coach, will you stop kicking the footballs into the lake?"

He just laughed and said, "You're not gonna find us a new coach, Harry. Just like you'll NEVER make a stupid video game. And your computer club is not gonna be around much longer, either. So NOBODY will be playing games when they should be practising. And by the way – we

haven't got a chance in the South-West Schools'
Cup, so you can forget that idea too. I heard
you tell your dad how we could do well in this
tournament and that's WHY he should come and
watch you. But if he ever turns up, I'm gonna
show him how GREAT you are at getting footballs
OUT OF THE LAKE – cos, basically, that's all you're
good for, cos you SUCK!"

Well, I'm going to show that idiot. Have you ever
played *FIFA 12*? Walnut's got it. It's OK but it
could do with some zombies. Anyway, you can
learn stuff from it, so I'm gonna learn how to
play, cos I figure, if I master *FIFA 12*, that's going
to make a BIG DIFFERENCE on the pitch!

Harry

From Charley **to** Harry
30 January 19:14 PST

Cuz –

Gaming is not the same as playing.

From Harry **to** Charley
31 January 07:16 GMT

That's why I talked to my dad and told him that
maybe him and me should start practising,
which he thought was some kind of joke, cos I've
never asked him to play football with me, EVER.
Anyway, we're going down to the village at the
weekend to use the pitch.

Pups – I'm in the village?
Where r u?
Harry

H – sorry. Looking at
pushchairs with yr mum.
Pups xxx

From Harry **to** Charley
01 February 20:58 GMT

Cuz –

Does your dad ever tell you he's gonna do sport with you and then he doesn't do it? Mine does, which, BTW, SUCKS.

HRH

HIS ROYAL HARRINESS

Tresinkum Farm

Cornwall PL36 0BH

2nd February

David Beckham

XIX Management

Unit 32/33

Ransomes Dock Business Centre

35–37 Parkgate Road

London SW11 4NP

Dear David Beckham, England's Greatest Dad
and Footballer, hi there,

My mum said, if there's one player in the whole

of England who could help turn me and my school team from a bunch of losers (no offence) into the best team in the South-West, it would be you. She said, if we had a parent like YOU involved in our school team, we wouldn't be the joke team everybody beats all the time.

I told my mum that's not going to happen because you don't live in Cornwall, you live in London. But my mum said you LOVE Cornwall. She said you even tried to buy a house down here. So that gave me a great idea!! Why don't you move your family to CORNWALL and live your CORNISH DREAM?!! Then you could send your kids to MY school. And I think your kid, Cruz, is about my age, so, if he's anything like you, we won't get slaughtered 10–2 every time we play St Brioc's (which, BTW, happened yesterday). And St Brioc's aren't even a GOOD team, but they are tough and ought to be kept in a zoo. Anyway, if we don't get better soon, we're gonna get hammered in the South-West Schools' Cup, which would NOT impress my friend, Jessica, who doesn't like losers.

When I told my mum I was going to write to you, she said, if you came to our matches, every mother at Mount Joseph's would turn up. I said, why? You're too old to play for our team. My mum said, believe me, the mums would come. And if the mothers arrived, Mount Joseph's would be a FORTRESS of screaming mums, which would really help us, cos it would INTIMIDATE our opponents, and give us a big HOME ADVANTAGE (which, BTW, we REALLY need).

Plus, I NEED some coaching with my football, cos my dad keeps standing me up when he tells me he's gonna help me out. So, if you have any Top Tips, feel free to pass 'em on. Our next taster day is in two weeks, time, which just happens to be when we have our first match of the tournament against Worthington Hall, so why don't you come down with Cruz, then I can tell Mr Phillips we have some real talent on the way and maybe – JUST MAYBE – we won't get CRUSHED in the first round (which doesn't really matter cos it's the group stages, not knockout). That's all I have to say.

Good luck and have fun and GBTM soon!

Harry Riddles

HIS ROYAL HARRYNESS

Tresinkum Farm
Cornwall PL36 0BH
2nd February

Alex Ferguson
Manchester United
Sir Matt Busby Way
Old Trafford
Manchester M16 0RA

Dear Sir Alex Ferguson, the greatest football
manager of all time, hi there,

I know you've won more trophies than any
other manager has EVER won in British history,

but there's one cup you missed – the South-West Schools' Cup! How would you like to help bring this cup home to Mount Joseph's?? Before you say yes, I should warn you that my school really sucks at football, and even miracle

workers like you can sometimes come unstuck when they see the SCALE of the miracle required. But if you fancy a new challenge and you're getting bored of being retired, let me know cos there might just be a job going, waiting for you here at Mount Joseph's! OK?

Good luck and have fun.

Harry Riddles

CHAPTER TEN
NEW BOOTS

Dad to Harry

After school today, yr mum and I have decided we're gonna get you a nice present for being so good about the twins, OK?
Dad

YAY!
Harry

From Harry **to** Charley
05 February 18:02 GMT

Dear Cuz –

How about this for bad luck. My dad takes me into town after school and tells me he wants to buy me a present for being such a good kid about these twins, so I think, GREAT! Until we walk into the SPORTS store. So I ask him what we're doing in R. J. Sports, when we should be over the street in Game World. He says, "We've come to get you that present we promised!"

I said, "Then we're in the wrong store!" He said, "We're not getting you a new game, Harry – we want to get you a new pair of FOOTBALL BOOTS!" I said, "Don't be crazy. I don't need new boots. But I DO need a new Xbox One!! Or *World of*

Zombies 3: Alien Resurrection!!"

He said, "Well, maybe if we BOUGHT you a nice pair of boots – like those orange ones up there – then it would INSPIRE you to start practising and playing more, and then you wouldn't be FIRST RESERVE, you'd be in the starting line-up!"

I said, "Firstly, if you want me to play more, then YOU'LL need to start playing with me, cos you NEVER show up when you say you will. And Walnut is never around in the evenings cos he's in surf club. And Charlotte HATES football. And Spencer only does what Charlotte WANTS him to do, so Dingbat is the only one I can rely on who ALWAYS wants to play football with me. But I don't learn much when I play with Dingbat because he just STEALS the football and then EATS IT!!! So, basically, I'm not really improving much and I don't see anything changing unless I find a person rather than a dog to practise with, so let's keep my old boots and get me that new game instead!"

Well, my dad looked a little bit upset and then he apologised and said he was really gonna try and make more of an effort to play with me. I told him he keeps telling me that, but he NEVER does it. But if he buys me the game, he won't have to feel guilty, cos there's ALWAYS somebody for me to play with online when he's not around.

Well, that got him, cos he said, "OK, if that's what

you really think, and that's what you want to do, then that's a shame, but I understand." So, just as we are about to head off across the street and buy *World of Zombies 3*, guess who walks in the store? Jessica. And that was it. I got snookered.

Harry

_____

From Charley **to** Harry
05 February 19:25 PST

Whaddya mean?

_____

From Harry **to** Charley
06 February 07:49 GMT

I mean Jessica came in the store and then I had

to introduce her to my dad. And my dad says, "Is this the Jessica you—". And I have to kick him so he doesn't go and embarrass me, but the damage is done and he starts smiling, cos my mum must have told him just how much I really like her.

Anyway, before he can ask her all the stupid stuff, Jessica asks him if we've come to buy me some new football boots. Then she said how cool it was to see me on the team and what a good idea it was to get me some boots, because every little advantage helps if we want to win that cup!

So my dad is just about to open his mouth, when I realise, if I don't say something now, what happens next could be the thing that kills ANY chance I EVER have of going out with her.

So, before my dad can tell her I don't want new football boots, but I DO want a new video game, I tell Jessica, "Yes! The reason we are in this SPORTS store was EXACTLY as you guessed!!! We are here to buy me a brand new pair of FOOTBALL BOOTS!!!"

Well, my dad just smiled and then I guess he thought it would be fun to tease me, so he says, "We can go over the street and get that game instead if you want, Harry?"

And for a split second I thought, Wait a minute. My dad just offered to buy me a VIDEO GAME. Maybe I should not look this gift horse in the mouth???

But then Jessica's mum walks in the store. She'd been parking the car and, as soon as she gets in the door, she starts telling Jessica how that kid Helmet has been in touch and how she's INVITED HIM TO STAY in the holidays!

Well, that did it. When I heard Mr I-know-all-these-great-ski-trails Helmet was going to be staying with Jessica and her mum and boasting about all his great sporting achievements, I said, "Forget the game, Pups. Let's get the boots!"

My dad looked real surprised but Jessica said, "Of course, Harry wants the boots! Right, Harry?" And that's when I put my big fat foot in it and said something that I think is gonna haunt me for the rest of my LIFE.

From Charley **to** Harry
06 February 07:52 PST

Whaddya say this time??

From Harry **to** Charley
06 February 21:48 GMT

I said, "With these boots, I'm gonna help Mount Joseph's win the South-West Schools' Cup!!!"

From Charley **to** Harry
07 February 08:00 PST

Well, that WAS dumb.

From Harry **to** Charley

07 February 20:59 GMT

I know – but what could I do?

From Charley **to** Harry

08 February 13:02 PST

Keep your mouth shut? That's what I would have done. Anyway, you didn't. So now you have MOUNTAINS to climb. And how do you plan on winning a tournament if you don't even PLAY football?

From Harry **to** Charley

08 February 21:04 GMT

Play more *FIFA*!!!

From Charley **to** Harry
08 February 13:16 PST

U r gonna need a LOT more than *FIFA* to win a football tournament.

From Harry **to** Charley
08 February 21:48 GMT

Jessica didn't think so. She said, "I'll bet Harry can do it!" And my dad looked at her as if she had a screw loose. But then I told her that me and my dad were gonna be working on some new stuff in the training ground, which we were gonna share with the team. And then we'd bring that cup home where it belongs! Mount Joseph's!

Well, my dad was kinda speechless, but Jessica's mum wasn't. She snorted, like the old dragon lady that she is, and said that was the most PREPOSTEROUS idea she'd ever heard and I was even more foolish than I looked if I thought our boys could POSSIBLY win that cup. Cos the Colts never win anything!!! Ever!!! Then she said, "And anyway, don't you just play computer games ,Harry?"

Well, that got my dad mad, but before he could jump in, I said, "Excuse me, I may enjoy playing the OCCASIONAL computer game, yes, but the reality is I LOVE PLAYING SPORTS!!"

Then, before my dad could say anything, I got us out of the store, cos I could see he wanted to give Jessica's mum a piece of his mind. So we left and, as we drove home, my dad asked me what kind of training-ground stuff I was thinking about, cos he didn't play much football growing up, as he was more of a skateboarder kind of kid. So I said, "I don't know much about football either, Dad, so I guess we'll both have to wing it and learn together!"

Then he asked me about the South-West Schools' Cup. Is it a big deal? I said, "It is now." And he said, "Well, maybe I've bitten off a little more than I can chew." And he may be right.

Night, Cuz.

_____

From Charley **to** Harry
08 February 16:15 PST

Squid –

My dad coaches our school lacrosse team. Maybe your dad can do something like THAT? So what if he doesn't play football? I don't think that guy José Mourinho, the manager of Chelsea, played football. But what you're gonna need is a GOOD coaching book and get him and you playing some pick-up games in your village with the local guys. Like I keep telling you, to get good at sport you have to practise, and then anything – ANYTHING – is possible. Even for a kid like you!

From Harry **to** Charley
10 February 16:16 GMT

Dear Cuz –

Thanks a lot for that vote of confidence. And I get it. Practice IS everything. That's probably why Ed Bigstock is taking Jessica up on Dartmoor next weekend, so he can give his dad's dogs some practice pulling his polar sled for the big expedition he is going to do when he walks to the North Pole again (which totally sucks, BTW – cos how am I gonna beat that for a ride? I don't have a polar sled. And Dingbat wouldn't pull one, even if I did!).

Anyway, I got other stuff to worry about. My headmaster collared me at lunch today and told me how he and the staff were really looking forward to seeing my new game – when was it going to be ready? I tried telling him we've had some glitches and it might be delayed for, like, another six or eight months or something, but he just laughed and said, "That's not what Ed Bigstock told me!" He said Ed said I'd invented this really cool game. And then he started tapping his palm with his finger and I said, "Oh, you mean, like, the tappy-tappy game?" And he said, "That's the one! The tappy-tappy game! Well, we can't WAIT to see it, Harry! Glitches, or no glitches! Why don't you give a presentation to the school the next time games are cancelled?"

I said, "But that could be tomorrow!"

And he said, "You've had PLENTY of time in the computer lab. I'm sure you've got some GREAT THINGS to show us!"

So now I have to show my school a game I haven't made – and all because of that idiot, Bigstock. And there's the football problem too. Cos Jessica asked me if I had told the team about how I was going to help give them that winning mentality that so far has been missing from every Colts XI team for, like, the last fifteen years!! So she hasn't forgotten about THAT!

Anyway, when I saw Bigstock later that day, he just laughed and said, "Can't wait to hear your training plans, Harry. I hear you and your dad have some GREAT NEW IDEAS for team tactics and football strategy that're going to turn this team around!! HA HA HA!!!"

I wish I hadn't opened my big mouth.

Harry

CHAPTER ELEVEN
DEAR LILY ALLEN

From Harry **to** Charley
16 February 14:03 GMT

Dear Cuz –

Guess what? My sister started using Twitter, cos
she thinks people are going to FOLLOW her. Last
night at dinner she was telling my mum and my
dad that every singer-songwriter who wants
to get ahead in the music business has to say
stuff on Twitter and have an Instagram account
to keep their fans interested in their incredible
life. I said, "What fans are we talking about? You
still haven't had your first gig!" (But this time I
ducked before she could hit me).

Anyway, on Saturday, Charlotte made my mum
drive her up to London to go to Oxford Street to
buy her an outfit for her first gig. But Charlotte

was scared sixteen hours in Topshop was NOT going to be enough time to find something to wear. So she had a huge fight with my dad the night before over money and shopping time and told him her best friend had just spent over eighty pounds on underwear from Victoria's Secret, so seventy pounds to spend at Topshop was PATHETIC. But my dad said, if she wants more money, then she can go earn it and he'll get her a job at the café on the beach, or down in the pub, washing glasses.

Well, that shut her up. Later, she came in my room and started going on about how nobody in this house cares about her any more, and that's why she has to move out and become famous, because only then will she find HAPPINESS!!

I didn't say anything, but this was like music to

my ears. I've spent YEARS trying to get rid of
that rattlesnake and now I realise all that
needed to happen was for my mum
and dad to go away on holiday,
have an 'accident', and then my
sister would WANT to pack
her bags and LEAVE. So
every cloud does have
a silver lining, after all.

Anyway, Charlotte's
first gig is coming up
tomorrow night. I'm just
hoping some talent scout decides to have a night
out at the surf club, spots Charlotte and gets her
to move up to London to be a STAR and then the
room problem is finally SOLVED.

Harry

HIS ROYAL HARRYNESS

Tresinkum Farm
Cornwall PL36 0BH
18th February

Lily Allen
Rocket Music Management
1 Blythe Road
London W14 0HG

Dear Lily Allen,

My sister, Charlotte, really wants to be a famous
pop star like you, but, between you and me, I
don't know if she's got it. Last night she had
her first gig at the surf club, but, just before my

mum turned up with the curry, she got a text from Spencer, who told her he didn't want them to be 'exclusive' any more.

Basically, this meant he wanted to go to parties without her and start seeing other girls. I can't say I blame him. Even though we call him the Living Dead, he's a good kid and puts up with A LOT going out with her. In fact, we were all pretty surprised he stayed with her as long as he did, cos she's pure evil.

Anyway, when he sends her this text, she goes NUTS!!! I mean, like, throwing stuff, kicking over chairs, having a total meltdown, until this other kid, Geoff, who has his own van and is a surfer, invites her to some party. My sister likes Geoff, cos he's fit and she says Spencer's a fat coach potato, but I don't like him cos he's a real jerk.

Anyway, she tells Pete, who runs the surf club, that she's gonna cancel her gig, cos she's too upset to sing now that she and Spencer have broken up. So Pete tells my mum, and my mum and Charlotte have this HUGE argument and then both of them start CRYING.

But that didn't stop my sister leaving. She said she'll never love anybody as much as she loved Spencer, and she was FAR too upset to SING. Then she jumped into Geoff's van and disappeared for the night. My mum said, with that attitude, she'll never make it, and that girl needs a mentor she RESPECTS. That's when I thought of you. Could you write to her and tell her to put her MUSIC before Geoff?

Good luck and have fun.

Harry Riddles

CHAPTER TWELVE
SUBSTITUTE OF THE MATCH

18 February 19:22 GMT

 Goofykinggrommet: You made yr game yet?

 Kid Zombie: Uh-uh.

 Goofykinggrommet: Whass goin' on?

 Kid Zombie: I wrote to the *FIFA* people and told 'em our idea. I said that guy Luis

Suarez would make a brilliant zombie cos he's always BITING people. Plus, my sister is a biter (but unfortunately she only plays hockey and NOT football). I said, if we could find a few more biters in the Premier League, *FIFA ZOMBIE* would not only be unbeatable, but completely BELIEVABLE!

Goofykinggrommet: They get back to you?

Kid Zombie: Nah. U gotta be thirteen to post on that forum, so I had to write snail mail and that could take months. But if they make that game, then you and me will be RICH!! And you know what else is pretty cool? My mum and dad said they're DEFINITELY gonna come to my next match so I can show 'em all the new moves I've learnt playing *FIFA*!

Goofykinggrommet: That will be, like, so cool!

 Kid Zombie: I know! When I tried my stuff out on Dingbat, he only got the ball once (but I got it back before he could eat it!), so I think I'm now ready.

From Harry **to** Charley
19 February 18:18 GMT

Dear Cuz –

Yesterday, we finally had our second match of the tournament (after three matches were cancelled by the floods). It was at home and we were doing pretty good, because Ed scored five goals before half-time. But the kids we played were ALMOST worse at football than us, so it's not THAT surprising that it was evens going into the second half – except they didn't have Bigstock on their team, and he was, like, on FIRE, which meant I only had to get the ball out the pond ONCE.

But I kept asking Mr Phillips if he could let me play, cos I had these new moves I wanted to try out, but Mr Phillips didn't want to put me on the pitch, until guess who FINALLY turned up to watch us play? MY MUM AND MY DAD!

As soon as they arrived, I knew EXACTLY what was going to happen. Mr Phillips would do what he always did when a parent showed up: he'd play their kid. ME! Yay!

From Charley **to** Harry
19 February 12.35 PST

Is this gonna end as bad as I think it will?

From Harry **to** Charley
19 February 18.52 GMT

Worse, maybe. Mr Phillips pulls off one of the

Tupolev brothers and puts me on in his place. So I get on the pitch and Bigstock comes running over and says, "You better not BLOW IT FOR US, HARRY!!"

But I wasn't listening to him, cos I was doing what Thierry Henry said he did before every game. Visualise what you are going to do on the pitch BEFORE you go out there, then DO IT. So I visualised how I was going to go out there and be SUBSTITUTE OF THE MATCH and I ignored that idiot Bigstock barking in my ear.

Well, that didn't work. We start playing and, the first time I get given a ball, I figure it's time for me to execute my Vieira pirouette, which, BTW, I make ten times out of ten on *FIFA*.

But when I TRY the Vieira, I stand on the ball, fall over, and they score again! And everybody starts laughing at me! So I think, Never mind. That was the lumpy pitch. I'll just play my Rivaldo turn instead, which will leave the opposition gasping in amazement. So next time I get the ball, I try my Rivaldo, lose the ball and – you guessed it – they SCORE AGAIN! Luckily, though, Bigstock kept scoring too, so the game was still tied up.

But now everybody is yelling at me to just pass the ball, or keep it, but not LOSE it. So I think, I can definitely do that. So we have, like, three minutes left and they make one last attack on our penalty area, when Bigstock strips the ball off one of them and passes to me and tells me to hit the ball to Oscar, up field.

So the ball comes over, I quickly scope Oscar, unload my right foot, but the ball SLICES off the side of my boot, goes BACK in the box, HITS Bigstock on the side of his BIG HEAD, and the ball rockets STRAIGHT back into OUR GOAL, giving

Bulmer no chance!!! So, like, me and Bigstock
had scored the winning goal – FOR THEM!!!

Well, I don't have to tell you what that was like.
I was DESTROYED. Any dreams I had of being
a footballer and helping Mount J's grab that
stupid little cup went straight out the window.
And when I looked over to see my mum and
dad... they'd gone. So I guessed they were too
embarrassed by my display. After the game,
even Jessica couldn't put a positive spin on it.
I think she tried to talk about the weather and
the terrible state of the football pitch, but I just
said, "It's not the pitch, Jessica, it's me. Bigstock
is right. So is my cousin. I don't know what I was
thinking."

She said, "You don't really suck, Harry. I know
you can do it. You just need more practice!" But

I think, after that performance, you're not gonna get me back out on a football pitch, cos it was TOO embarrassing.

Harry

From Charley **to** Harry
19 February 19:15 PST

Cuz –

So you're gonna quit just like that after one bad day at the office?? I thought you told Jessica you were going to win that cup for Mount Joseph's. Or did you forget about that?

CHAPTER THIRTEEN
ZOMBIE SHOWJUMPING

Dear Cuz –

This evening I had a GREAT idea. I told my mum
I'm going to move out and spend this weekend
in our old CARAVAN (you know the one my mum
sometimes uses as an office? That one). Then, if
I like it, we WON'T have to get an extension. And
those stupid twins can HAVE my stupid room. And
NOBODY will get mad. Plus (and this is a pretty
COOL plus), who's going to stop me from GAMING?

Nobody. Not if it means they have to walk across
the yard in the middle of the night when it's
raining, right?

My friend Walnut lives in his caravan in the

summer when his mum and dad do B&B. He says he LOVES it out there, so that's what I'm gonna try too.

Plus, the headmaster is definitely going to shut my computer club down if I don't show him my new game, cos Mr Phillips told him that Bulmer, Oscar and me spend all our free time in the computer room and that's why he never sees us down on the training pitch practising after school. But are you surprised after what happened to me last time?

Harry

From Charley **to** Harry
20 February 19:19 PST

Smurf –

You want to move into a mobile home? U
crazy? It's the middle of WINTER!!!

Charley

I know, but I need to make plans, cos 17th May is coming fast and my mum and dad have said they can't afford a new extension. So, for the first few months, the twins will be in with them, but, after that, they'll need to figure out something, or those kids will be in my bed – which I definitely DON'T want.

Harry

22 February 21:42 GMT

 Goofykinggrommet: Harry - you in yr caravan?

 Kid Zombie: Uh-huh!

 Goofykinggrommet: How is it?

 Kid Zombie: OMG - it's SO cool. U gotta come for a sleepover here! It's, like, so

Goofykinggrommet: So what?

 Kid Zombie: I think there's somebody OUTSIDE!!!! Wait a minute!!!!

 Goofykinggrommet: What do you mean?

 Kid Zombie: OMG. There's... HELPPPPPPPPP!

 Goofykinggrommet: Harry? Harry, what's going on?

 Goofykinggrommet: Harry, u there?

 Kid Zombie: OMG - there's WRITING!!! On my WINDOW! Looks like it's in BLOOD!!!!! I GOTTA GET OUTTA HERE!!!!

From Charley **to** Harry
23 February 11:18 PST

Noodge –

My mom just told me what happened with
you in the caravan. Ha ha, that's pretty
funny. Your sister needs to be put on a chain
and locked in a box. So what are you gonna
do? You gonna go back out there again now
you know there is no bogeyman, just your
stupid sister and her new boyfriend? He
sounds like a creep, BTW.

Charley

From Harry **to** Charley
24 February 19:20 GMT

He is. He said writing that stuff on the caravan window in fake blood was a joke. But I didn't find it FUNNY. I'm now thinking Spencer wasn't such a bad kid, after all. At least he was a nice guy. This guy is always smacking me on the head and telling me to pull his stupid finger.

The only good news is he wants to be a plumber and move to Australia and get rich, so – who knows? – maybe he'll take Charlotte with him. Anyway, next time I see Spencer, I'm telling him to give her a second chance. I'll even let him use my Xbox if he starts dating her again.

Still, at least one good thing happened to me today. I KNOW WHAT GAME TO MAKE! Jessica caught me coming out the computer room playing the bird game on my phone and said how she wished there was a showjumping game, cos then she'd DEFINITELY want to play it. So I showed her the flappy bird game on my phone and she said, "This is, like, SO fun – but where's the pony?"

And that made me think: a horse! Change the flappy bird to a horse! And maybe put a ZOMBIE on his back to make him look cool! Then, instead of him FLYING through posts, I'll get the horse and zombie to JUMP over the posts by tapping the screen. How about that for a cool game?

Harry

CHAPTER FOURTEEN
JESSICA'S GAME

24 February 20:27 GMT

 Kid Zombie: Guy Fox? You online?

 Guy Fox: Hey, Harry – long time no see.
What's up?

 Kid Zombie: Ah, you know. Nothing.
Home. Usual.

 Guy Fox: Whaddya want?

Kid Zombie: U know that thing we talked about?

 Guy Fox: What thing?

 Kid Zombie: That game thing.

 Guy Fox: You mean the game code thing?

 Kid Zombie: Yeah, yeah. The game code thing. I think I'd really like it.

 Guy Fox: Sure. No problem. But u can only re-skin the game at yr school, Harry. Otherwise, there's no way this is going to work.

Kid Zombie: OK, so if you send it to me at school, I can do it, right?

Guy Fox: Probably take you half an hour, maybe an hour, max. A baby could do it. What are you going to put in its place?

Kid Zombie: A pony and a zombie.

Guy Fox: A pony and a zombie? OK. Send me the game when you're done.

Kid Zombie: I will! Thanks!

From guyfox@mickeymouse.com
to harry.riddles@mountjosephschool.co.uk
Subject: bird source code
25 February 13:02 GMT

Kid Zombie –

Open and enjoy, my friend!

Guy Fox.

OMG, Cuz – help!
Harry

What have you done now?
Charley

I'm in big
TROUBLE!!!

What's new?

From Harry **to** Charley

25 February 20:08 GMT

No, but this time it's really serious. Remember I
told you I met this kid online who said he could
help me out with some gaming code? Well, he
sent me the code at school and I opened the
install package and in, like, ten minutes I had this
new game up and running, which looked super
cool.

So I went and got Bulmer, and Bulmer LOVED
the game. Then Bigstock showed up. Bigstock
wanted to know what everyone was getting
so excited about. So Bulmer tells Bigstock I've
made this AMAZING new game, and Bigstock
grins and says he's going to tell the headmaster –
which I thought was kind of weird, cos normally
Bigstock would be, like, "You're a loser, your game

sucks, don't bother showing it to anybody, blah, blah, blah, blah, blah." But he was, like, "Oh, that's a really interesting game, Harry!! Let me get the headmaster and you can give us all a demonstration!"

So he got the headmaster and I showed him my new game and he asked me if I can do a demo on a screen in the assembly room after lunch. He said, "This will be a TREAT for the students to see what GREAT THINGS you've managed to make here in the computer club! It may even inspire MORE students to sign up for a computer science course! Well done, Harry!"

So I'm feeing pretty good about this, until Bigstock laughs and says, "This is going to be hilarious!" Which didn't sound good.

Anyway, that afternoon, I'm standing in front of the whole school, and everything is hooked up to my phone, where the game is loaded and ready to play, and so I say, "OK, everybody – here's my new game!" Just before I hit PLAY, Bulmer asks me what I'm going to call it. And I think about it and, before I can stop myself, I say, "I'm calling it 'Jessica's Game'." Cos she gave me the idea. And I look at Jessica and she kind of blushes, but I think she was pleased cos not many people make you your own game, right?

Anyway, then I hit PLAY and up on the big screen the zombie and the pony come riding across the screen, just like they are meant to. And I tap the screen. And my horse and zombie jump over one post. So I tap it again. And they jump over another post. And everybody in the school goes *ooh* and *aaah* and I'm thinking, This is so GREAT! Until the horse just gallops straight OUT OF THE PICTURE!!!

So now I'm thinking, Well, that was NOT meant to happen. I keep tapping my screen and then suddenly the big screen goes *POP*! And all the lights in the school go OUT!! And the fire alarm goes OFF!!! All at the same time!!! And now I'm thinking, Didn't we just have this new internet system installed that controls all that school stuff? This better not have anything to do with THAT!!!

The headmaster starts scratching his head and TWO minutes later there's POLICE sirens and FIRE ENGINES coming up the school drive! So now I'm thinking, OMG, I hope this has got nothing to do with ME!

It turns out the police got an SOS call that the school had flooded and kids were trapped in classrooms and it was a major disaster area at Mount Joseph's. So the headmaster had to go outside to tell them there was no flood, and nobody was trapped in the classrooms, and no one from the office had called the emergency services, so it must be a FALSE ALARM.

But they say that they got an alarm call from a mobile phone and they show my headmaster the number. So he comes in the hall and asks us if anybody has this number. And, guess what?

It's MY NUMBER!!! So I put my hand up and the headmaster tells me to come out and talk to the police.

So I go outside and they ask me if I called them and I say, "No, I was giving a gaming demo to the school." So the policeman asks to see my phone and he flicks through my apps and shows me I have this new app on my phone called SOS DISTRESS. I said I never downloaded SOS DISTRESS. And I never pranked the police cos I would never do that!

Anyway, he starts scrolling through the history and he finds there was an SOS sent to the fire and police requesting immediate emergency assistance and this was sent 12 minutes earlier – which was when I was giving my demo. I said, "But I didn't SEND an SOS!! All I did was press PLAY on my new game!" So he said it came from my phone so somehow I DID SEND IT. Even if I didn't MEAN to send it.

So, anyway, that's how my game demo to the school ended – with half of Devon and Cornwall's police and emergency services parked in front of the school and me in trouble for pranking the police.

CHAPTER FIFTEEN
FALLOUT KID

From Harry **to** Charley
26 February 18:52 GMT

Cuz –

Guy Fox has definitely done something to our computers. You know what happened to the third form in IT today? All the computers suddenly STOPPED working as word processors and then started working like the *Pac-Man* computer game (which, BTW, the third formers LOVED!). So Mr Green then pulled the plug and had all the computers taken away to get inspected. So now we have NO computers at school and I think it's probably MY fault.

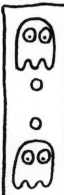

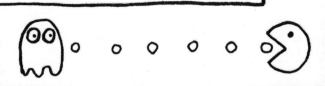

From Charley **to** Harry
26 February 18:06 PST

Tell your dad what happened.

From Harry **to** Charley
27 February 07:32 GMT

But he'll KILL ME! And, anyway, when I got
home my mum sent me this email from the
headmaster's office, asking me if I know anything
about it. What do you think?

From The headmaster, John Forbes (j.f@mountjosephschool.co.uk) **to** Wilson & Rita Riddles (and 110 others)
Subject: My Birthday!!!

Dear Parents,

As you may or may not know, it's my BIRTHDAY next week and I would like to invite you all to a special party here at the school! Fancy dress ONLY.
Theme: Mount Joseph's TRANSFORMERS!

Please send a cheque of at least £250 to my secretary and mark it John Forbes Birthday Party Fund! Look forward to seeing you in your robot suits. But gentlemen, please – no Optimus Prime – that bad boy is mine! RSVP.

John Forbes

From Charley **to** Harry
26 February 23:38 PST

What's wrong with that? Optimus Prime is definitely the most kick-ass Transformer!

From Harry **to** Charley
27 February 07:41 GMT

My mum says, even though my headmaster is under a lot of pressure after the emergency services prank, he's not crazy. You don't ask parents for money for your own birthday party, unless you're their kid! And dressed as Optimus Prime? I doubt Mr Forbes even knows who Optimus Prime is. And, anyway, she says his birthday is in September.

From Harry **to** Charley
27 February 21:10 GMT

Cuz –

This is just getting worse. At assembly this morning, the headmaster asked if anybody was responsible for sending out a hoax email to all the parents inviting them to his birthday party. Nobody put their hand up. So then he asked if anybody knew about the delivery of £3000 pounds' worth of fireworks for this party? Still nobody put their hand up. Finally, he said, "Then presumably nobody knows who sent out an email to ALL the parents telling them that our school term was going to be cut short by two weeks in order to have a cockroach infestation problem seen to by our local pest control unit?"

"Three cheers, for Mr Forbes!" shouted Ed Bigstock. But Mr Forbes gave him a detention for being cheeky. And THAT'S when he looked over at me and said, "Harry – my office. Five minutes, please." Which made me feel pretty sick.

So I'm waiting for the hall to empty and it's just me left in the room, with all those huge oil paintings up on the walls of famous old Mount Joseph pupils (who didn't get kicked out for crashing the school computer network) and then Jessica walks past, but she doesn't look at me, or say anything, and, before I can talk to her, the headmaster calls me into his study.

So I go in and Mr Forbes says, "Look, Harry – I know you wouldn't do something like this on purpose, but how did you get that game?" I tell him everything and he thanks me for being honest, but tells me I'm in SERIOUS trouble, and he will need time to consider what PUNISHMENT I deserve. So why don't I go away and have a think about what I did? And then he'll have a think about what I did. And then we should meet with my PARENTS and possibly the POLICE and decide what to do with ME!! And I thought, Police? I don't want to go to jail!

As soon as I got out of that room, I called my mum and got really upset. Then matron found me and said not to worry. Everything was going to be all right. It probably wasn't ME who crippled the school computer network. And it probably wasn't MY fault that Mr Phillip's sports car got filled with water accidentally by one of the fire engines. And just because everyone on the board of governors had to change ALL their home numbers, their bank details, and their email addresses, it probably wasn't MY fault. Then she gave me a hug and asked me if I was feeling any better now that we'd had a little talk. But you know what? I didn't.

So I got home and then we had a big FAMILY MEETING and I told my mum and dad what happened and they were pretty nice about it, but they said the internet is not a toy and you have to be careful who you talk to, or you can get in a LOT of trouble. In the meantime, they were going to stop me from going online for a while (except emails). So my life sucks. And to make things WORSE, my dad has given me these two stupid soccer movies to watch.

Harry

CHAPTER SIXTEEN
UNI

From Harry **to** Charley
02 March 19:21 GMT

Dear Cuz –

Now that I've been banned from just about everything and my life at my school hangs by a thread, and the twins are arriving soon and will probably need my room, I've been thinking there's an easy way out of all of this that will save everybody a LOT of energy working out what to do with me. I thought, with my grades, maybe I could come to college with you? As an early student kind of thing? I know some kids of twelve have gone to Oxford University, so this isn't completely crazy, and I was getting pretty decent grades before all this happened. So here's my application. Please look through it and tell me what you think.

UNIVERSITY OF DENVER COLLEGE APPLICATION

**Todd Rinehart, Associate Vice Chancellor for
Enrollment and Director of Admissions,
University of Denver,
2199 S. University Blvd.
Denver,
CO 80208**

Thank you for starting your Pioneer Application to the
University of Denver!

We've sent your login information to the email address
you provided, should you need to save and return to
your application.

Get started now!

First name:
Harry

Last name:
Riddles

Email address:
harryriddles1@gmail.com

Gender:
Male

Place of birth:
Treliske Hospital, Truro, Cornwall

What is your country of citizenship?
England

What is your visa type?

My family are STILL waiting for your President to help us out on that one, so my visa type is, I don't know.

Optional information:

Do you intend to apply for need-based financial aid by submitting an FAFSA and PROFILE (all students are considered for merit aid during the admission review process)?

You bet. The pocket money I get does not pay for everything I need. Plus, I don't know how thrilled my dad will be when I tell him I'm leaving Mount Joseph's and going to college in Denver with my big cousin.

Tell us more about your education:

Basically, my education is GREAT! My mum or my

dad drives me and my sister to school and we try and get there by 8.25 (unless the car breaks down). Then I have lessons until one, which can be kind of boring if it's Thursday when we have double P.E., but great on Wednesdays when we have double I.T. Then we have lunch. Then we have two more lessons after lunch. Then we have sports. EVERY DAY.

High school information:
Mount Joseph's School

Your guidance counselor:
Please provide the following information about your high school guidance counselor. Once you submit your application, an email will be sent to your counselor alerting him or her to the steps required to help you complete your application.

Counselor first name:
Mr Phillips

Counselor email address:
peter.p@mountjosephschool.co.uk

BTW – do you really need to get in touch with him? His old sports car got flooded by one of the fire engines, and he blames me. Same with the guinea pigs that Guy Fox got delivered to his house as a stupid joke.

Have you enrolled in any college-level courses?
Not yet.

College plans:
What are you interested in studying? If you're not sure, that's OK; just select 'Undeclared.'

I'm interested in studying how to get RICH, STAY OUT OF TROUBLE, and make life EASIER for everybody (including me).

Activities:
Please list your activities in order of importance and/or most significant time commitment.

Activity/Work experience:
1 *World of Zombies*. In the good old days, fifteen hours a week (but now zero).
2 TV. Approximately six hours a week (but we watch a LOT of movies).
3 Homework. Normally done in the break before I have to give it in (now that my dad doesn't have time to help me with it).
4 Walking Dingbat. Every day, thirty minutes per day during the week. Plus, the w/e. (More if I get paid. Or my dad is away, cos

nobody else can be bothered to walk him.)
5 Football practice, which, BTW, I've just
   started to do more of, cos I want to prove
   to Jessica that I'm not just a dumb gamer
   kid who causes lots of trouble and makes
   everybody mad. Plus, I've got nothing else
   I'm allowed to do any more.

Leadership positions held:

I set up my own gaming site, so I guess I'm
head of the school computer club. Also, I'm first
reserve for Mount Joseph's Colts XI. I am also the
number two shooter for my age in the *World of
Zombies* gamer chart (which is pretty AWESOME,
BTW).

Let's finish up!

After you hit 'submit', we'll guide you through your
next steps:

Paying your application fee.
How much are we talking about?

Sending your test scores to DU.
I don't have test scores, but I can send you my
school reports (but maybe best not look at the
end of THIS term report, cos I have a feeling my
headmaster is not gonna be so nice after all the
trouble with Guy Fox).

But first, we have to ask –
Have you ever been found responsible for
a disciplinary violation at an educational
institution you have attended from the 9th
grade (or international equivalent) forward,
whether related to academic misconduct or
behavioral misconduct, that resulted in your
probation, suspension, removal, dismissal, or
expulsion from the institution?

Tough one. I did get in trouble for this prank
I played on Ed Bigstock in Latin, but the kid
deserved it. Then there's this other thing that's
not really a big deal, but it was kinda my fault.
So maybe we could just skip that one, OK? Thanks
a lot!

Have you been convicted of a misdemeanor, felony, or other crime?

Not yet, but we're meeting with the police on
Tuesday, so I don't know how that's going to
turn out.

Make it OFFICIAL –

I certify that the information on this application
is complete and correct, and I understand that the
submission of false information is grounds for denial of
my application, withdrawal of any offer of acceptance,

cancellation of enrollment, or any appropriate
disciplinary action.

I do. OK? When do I start?

Harry Riddles

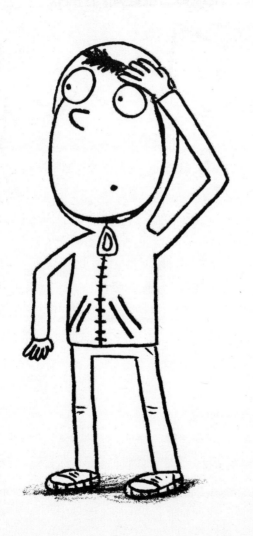

CHAPTER SEVENTEEN
PUBLIC ENEMY
NUMBER ONE

From Charley **to** Harry
03 March 21:03 PST

Did they catch Guy Fox?

From Harry **to** Charley
04 March 07:14 GMT

No – he's using some server you can't trace,
so they don't think they'll ever catch him.
Anyway, me and my mum are going in to see the
headmaster tomorrow, so I don't know what's
going to happen. Maybe I'll be excluded.

Harry

From Charley **to** Harry
03 March 23:16 PST

Everything will be OK. Wasn't yr fault.

_____

From Harry **to** Charley
04 March 07:57 GMT

That's not what everybody at school is saying.
We're meeting Forbes today. Will write when I
get home.

Pups – HEEEEEELPPPPP!!! Me and mum on way 2 HOSPITAL!!! Think mum HAVING twins!! Call meeeee!!!!
Harry

Can't call. In hospital. They got mum with the doctors. Dunno what's happening!!! Come quick!!!
Harry

Here's doctor!! Gotta go!!!
Harry

From Charley **to** Harry
04 March 08:16 PST

Cuz –

My dad said you had a big emergency with
your mum. You OK? What happened?

Charley to Harry

Cuz –
You OK? GBTM.
Charley

From Harry **to** Charley
04 March 22:14 GMT

Dear Cuz –

This was the WORST DAY OF MY LIFE. Mum picks
me up from school, and we head off for a drive
and a 'chat' cos we couldn't see the headmaster
till 5.30. But I could tell my mum was really
worried about what was going to happen to me,
and when we're driving she starts holding her
belly and telling me the twins seem restless
and maybe we need to think about getting to
the hospital.

So she takes this short cut down this valley and,
after we cross this river ford, which was, like,
FULL of rainwater, our car STOPS. For NO reason.
And it won't start again!

So I try calling my dad. And then I call the emergency services, but I have no signal, and it's suddenly like this BIG emergency, cos I ask my mum if she's OK and she says, "NO! We need HELP!" But when she got out the car, she said she couldn't walk anywhere. So it was up to ME! Then she told me to run and find help, but be QUICK, cos we didn't have much TIME cos the twins wanted to get BORN!!!

So I didn't know what to do or where to go, but then I thought if I could just get HIGH enough, MAYBE I could get a signal! So I found this super tall tree, but I don't like heights, cos they really scare me. So I look up at this tree and it, like, goes up, and up, and UP. And I think, If I could climb it, I would definitely get a signal, but it's, like, OMG, that's one of the tallest trees I've EVER seen!!! But what else can I do? I HAD to do it.

So I start climbing. And I don't look down. I just keep going up. And a couple of times I nearly fell when I slipped off the branch and it was, like, the scariest thing I've ever had to do in my whole life, and when I finally reached the top I pulled out my phone and almost dropped it, but I grab it, look at it and FINALLY I see I have a signal. But then I thought, Wait a minute – I don't know where we are! How am I going to tell them how to FIND US?

But then I remember that creep, Guy Fox, and the not-so-stupid SOS app he put on my phone,

which gives the EXACT GPS location of where I am! So I used that and, like, ten minutes later they sent us an AIR AMBULANCE. So, OMG, cuz. WHAT A DAY!!!

From Charley **to** Harry
04 March 17:04 PST

Nice catch, Smurf! What happened at the hospital?

From Harry **to** Charley
05 March 07:18 GMT

There were, like, THREE doctors and a nurse waiting to look after my mum, who was, like, groaning and unable to talk. So they took her inside and I didn't know if she was going to be all right or not. One of the doctors who brought my mum in asked me if I was OK, but I couldn't talk. He said I did a really good job climbing up that tree and having that useful app on my phone. I said, "If it wasn't for me making her upset, maybe none of this would have happened." He said, "Don't worry, son; let's call your dad." So we did and, a while later, my dad turned up with Charlotte and Geoff. I wanted to stay near my mum, but my dad said only one person was allowed to stay, so me and Charlotte and Geoff came home. They kept her in over night, so we're gonna go and see her today again after school. I just hope she's OK.

———————————————————

From Charley **to** Harry
05 March 10:20 PST

Good job, kid. Let me know what happens.

From Harry **to** Charley
05 March 21:20 GMT

Cuz –

We went to hospital after school and I put on these earphones and you know what I heard? Heartbeats! From the little twins! It was, like, so INCREDIBLE. My mum said, "That's cos of YOU, Harry!! You saved them! What a great big brother you are!"

And when she said that it was, like, wow – these little twins are my new family. How cool is that?!

And you know what else is cool? I'm not getting evil sisters like Charlotte. I'm getting some little BROTHERS!!! YAY!!!

Harry

CHAPTER EIGHTEEN
SMUGGLERS' TUNNEL

HIS ROYAL HARRINESS

Tresinkum Farm
Cornwall PL36 0BH
16th March

The Duke and Duchess of Cambridge
Clarence House
London SW1A 1BA

Dear The Duke and Duchess of Cambridge, hi
again,

I wrote to you a while back about my evil sister,
Charlotte, to see if you wanted to give her a real
job. So thanks a lot for writing back to me and
you probably made a very SMART choice not
taking her on, cos she is a bit of a nightmare.

Plus, she's just got this new boyfriend, so I don't think she'd take the job even if you gave it to her.

Anyway, the reason I'm writing again is cos of my mum. She's gonna be stuck in hospital for AGES cos of these twins. But she's told me she's really BORED and HOMESICK. Did you have that problem in hospital when you had the Prince? Or did the Duke come in and tell some jokes? My dad sucks at telling jokes. I like that one that goes, What do you call an alligator in a vest? An Investigator! Or, What do lawyers wear to court? Lawsuits! But my mum has heard my

jokes a million times, so if you have any other good jokes, can you please send them? And if you know any famous comics who might want to play a gig in a hospital, can you give 'em my address and ask them to get in touch? I know Cornwall is a long way to come, but it will be worth it, cos my mum says there're lots of old people there who need cheering up and are really nice.

That's all I have to say. Good luck and have fun.

Harry Riddles

OMG – guess who just arrived
at my house? Jessica!
Harry

Jess frm yr skool?
Walnut

Yeah!!!

From Mum **to** Harry

22 March 18:43 GMT

My little hero –

Your dad tells me you had a surprise visitor this afternoon. How did that go?

Mum xxx

From Harry **to** Mum

22 March 19:01 GMT

Good, maybe.

From Mum **to** Harry

22 March 19:18 GMT

What's that mean?

From Harry **to** Mum
22 March 19:21 GMT

I dunno. I mean, it started gr8. Then not so gr8.

_____

From Mum **to** Harry
22 March 19:27 GMT

How come?

_____

From Harry **to** Mum
22 March 19:52 GMT

Well, she came over to see how I was, cos everybody in my school is down on me for all that Guy Fox stuff. But, you know what was really cool? She found me practising FOOTBALL

in our barn, which was something she wasn't
expecting cos she thought I'd be gaming. So
then she tells me that she plays football in some
girls' league at the weekends – but she doesn't
like talking about it. So we start kicking the ball
around and she's, like, UNBELIEVABLE. I mean,
like, almost as good as Bigstock! So we played in
the barn until Geoff turned up and wanted me to
pull his stupid finger.

We had, like, an hour before her mum was going to pick her up, so I said, "Why don't you come and see a smugglers' tunnel?" So I took her down the valley and, when we got down the bottom by the stream, I showed her the hole in the side of the hill, which BTW is now REALLY overgrown with long grass. But she was SO excited to find a real smugglers' tunnel – which was cool, cos I thought she'd think it was, like, too SCARY or something.

So then she asked me HOW I found this tunnel and I told her you guys knew about it and we came here all the time in the summer, when all the other beaches in Cornwall were PACKED. Cos the only way you can get to this beach is by this old tunnel. Or by boat. So it was, like, a SECRET beach.

From Mum **to** Harry
22 March 20:01 GMT

Was she OK? That tunnel is v tight in places.

From Harry **to** Mum
22 March 20:15 GMT

Mum, she LOVED the tunnel!

I didn't tell her it was maybe 150 metres long and sometimes it would get REALLY narrow, and REALLY wet, and REALLY slippery, but I did say she might find it scary, so, if she wanted to, we could go back to the house and play. But she said she didn't want to go back, cos this was a GREAT ADVENTURE!!!

So I used the torch on my phone, and me and Dingbat and her slithered and crawled and slipped and slid, which was basically pretty good fun, but, you know what it's like, it's at least ten minutes before you start to see some light from the beach, so you could easily get scared, but she DIDN'T.

And when we got down to the beach, Jessica told me that going down that old tunnel was WAY more exciting than dog sledding over Dartmoor with Ed. So that made me feel pretty good.

From Mum **to** Harry
22 March 20:25 GMT

That sounds perfect, Harry! What went wrong?

From Harry **to** Mum
22 March 20:41 GMT

Well, me and her were sitting up on a big rock,
listening to some music on my phone and

watching these HUGE waves come in, and then she held my arm, which made me feel pretty good until Helmet sent her a text. So it was ALMOST the best day

Going to bed now.

Love you, Mum.

Harry xxxxxxxxx

Dear Cuz –

I've been talking to the boyz about yr little
problem and we have some advice for you.
Don't go into the headmaster's office and
roll over like a beaten dog begging for mercy,
cos that never works. Your best form of
DEFENCE is to go on the OFFENCE. You
know what I mean? Go in there with a game
plan and tell him how you're gonna make
things right for YOU and YOUR SCHOOL.
Then you might have a chance. Let me know
how it goes.

Charley

Jessica to Harry

Dear Harry – Thank you very much for the BEST DAY EVER! I'm sending you a present (which I hope you'll like). Good luck with the headmaster next week. Jessica x

OMG, Jessica – I had the best day TOOOOOO!!! And u don't have to send me a present, but, if you did, that would be pretty gr8! Can't WAIT to see u at skool!!!! Harry xxxxxxxxxxxxxxxxxxxxxxxxxxxxxxxxxxxx xx xxxxxxx xxxxxxxx

(Not sent)

Dear Jessica – I'm glad you had such a good day. I WOULD have had a good day if that IDIOT HELMET hadn't txtd u. Harry x

(Not sent)

Dear Jessica – I had a really gr8 day 2 and can't wait to see u at skool. So thanks for coming by. BTW – u rock at football and I'm gonna tell Ed he's got competition! Love Harry xxx

CHAPTER NINETEEN

COACH DAD

Charley to Harry

Cuz –
U gonna be home schooled?
What did they give you?
Charley

No home schooling, but guess what?
I GOT A TEXT FROM JESSICA.
Harry

Is that all u can think about?
What happened with the head?

Good. Maybe. I don't know.

What happened???

From Harry **to** Charley
25 March 20:08 GMT

Well, basically, me and my dad went in to see him, and I thought about all that stuff you told me. But before I could even open my mouth, the headmaster told us how I'd caused A LOT of TROUBLE and EXPENSE and how this was a VERY SERIOUS MATTER INDEED. So not the best start, if you know what I mean.

But then he said he quite liked my little zombie game thingummy... until the fire brigade turned up. And the car got filled up with water. And all that other stupid stuff happened. But SOME of the parents had written to the board of governors telling them they had to make an EXAMPLE of me after their home computers started glitching cos of the Guy Fox birthday email thing.

But he said he also had some letters from some kids at my school (Jessica and Bulmer), who wrote some good things about me, which was a BIG help to him. He said he wasn't exactly SURE what Bulmer wrote, cos Bulmer's writing was almost unreadable, but Jessica's letter was very sensible. She told him I was making a big effort to get more involved in school activities, like computer club, and sports, and that I should be given a SECOND CHANCE.

So then he asked me if I was sorry. I said, "I never would have done it if I knew THIS was going to happen." He said, "It would be a great shame to lose you, Harry. But I have to do SOMETHING!!"

And this is when I pulled my rabbit out of my hat and did what you SAID I should do. Which, BTW, was a VERY BIG DEAL for me.

And VERY SCARY too, cos I don't normally do this kind of thing. But I figured, if I didn't, I might not have a school to go to.

From Charley **to** Harry
25 March 19:29 PDT

What did you say?

From Harry **to** Charley
26 March 07:43 GMT

I said, "I understand why everybody's mad with me, but I've got this GREAT idea for a punishment!" So the headmaster asks, "What might this be?" And I say, "Well, since Mr Phillips has to go back home to New Zealand, we're going to need a NEW coach for the next two weeks of the tournament." So the headmaster says, "Where are you going with this, Harry?

So I bring out this book I have in my pocket, called *Training to Win!* which was this book Jessica sent me as a present after I took her down the smugglers' tunnel. So I give it to him and he opens the book and sees the note from Jessica, which said, "I use this book all the time, Harry. I know it will help you a lot!! Love Jessica x"

Then I say, "How about we come to an arrangement? What if I help Mount Joseph's WIN the South-West Schools' Cup, then you give me a SUSPENDED sentence? That way I give something BACK to the school: WINNING! And you give me a SECOND CHANCE! How about that for a GREAT idea?"

From Charley **to** Harry
26 March 07:42 PDT

That's pretty wild. He go for it?

_____

From Harry **to** Charley
26 March 21:04 GMT

He says, "YOU want to coach the school team?"

I say, "*I* can't coach the team! Nobody will listen to me! Plus, how am I going to drive the school bus to games? I CAN'T! But I know somebody who CAN! And who would make a MOST EXCELLENT coach!" And my dad says, "And who might this be, Harry?" So I point to my dad and say, "You, Pups!!!"

 Well, both the headmaster AND my dad are, like, SPEECHLESS, cos I don't think either of them were expecting me to come out with that idea! But I figured, if I could get my school to WIN something for the first time in DECADES, that's got to make the board of governors, AND the grumpy parents, and the headmaster more willing to let me stay at my school. Cos who wants to send their kids to a school for losers? Even if it's a GREAT school!!! Plus, me and my dad would make a GREAT coaching team!!!

From Charley **to** Harry
26 March 18:20 PDT

Nice! What did yr dad say?

From Harry **to** Charley
27 March 07:40 GMT

He said he'd think about it. So I said, "What do you mean, you'll think about it? You HAVE to do it, Dad, cos then we can hang out together! And you haven't been there for me ALL TERM! Plus, I thought you WANTED a footballer son? So what's two weeks of just you and me doing something really cool and SPORTY together? I really need this to work."

I didn't say any more, but I could tell Dad was really thinking about everything I'd said, and he was looking at me with this kind of sad look on his face, and then he just nodded and said he'd give the headmaster his decision by the end of the week. And that's where we are. In LIMBO. And the tournament starts again in, like, eight days and there are lots of parents already moaning that they've booked holidays and they might yank their kids from the team, cos this tournament was meant to finish during the school term!!!

From Charley **to** Harry
27 March 21:50 PDT

But the rule is, sports comes first, second and third, or you come last! Even during the holidays! No wonder you guys never win the World Cup!

Yr cuz,

Charley (aka the MVP Guy!!!)

CHAPTER TWENTY
THE MASTER PLAN

Dear Harry – How did it go with the headmaster? R u coming bk to skool nxt term? I hope so. Plz txt me.
Jess xxx

Dear Jessica – I will DEFINITELY be coming back. Me and my dad r coaching the Colts for the rest of the tournament!!!!
Harry XXXXXXXXXXXXX

OMG – great!!! How's it going?

Always raining. Pitch always flooded. Hardly anybody turns up, but I have a MASTER PLAN!

Whass that?

Zombies!

29 March 14:22 GMT

 Kid Zombie: Walnut - what's up?

 Goofykinggrommet: HARRY! OMG - what r u doing back on *WoZ*? I thought ur parents banned you?

 Kid Zombie: They did - until all this rain ruined our team practices cos all the pitches at my school are flooded!

Goofykinggrommet: So why u on *WoZ*?

 Kid Zombie: Cos I told my dad that playing *WoZ* was possibly the ONLY way to get our team playing like a team, since nobody turns up for practice.

 Goofykinggrommet: U told him playing video games was gonna help you play football like a team?

 Kid Zombie: Yeah.

 Goofykinggrommet: And he went for it?

 Kid Zombie: He didn't have a lot of choice. Most Mount Joseph's parents do NOT want their kids spending the school holidays at Mount Joseph's. So they don't show up for fitness training. Or shooting drills. Or dead ball practices. Or all the other stuff that me and my dad figured we needed to practise to give us a chance at playing better. And my dad was, like, pulling his hair out and THAT'S when I had my great idea. So I said, "Every kid on the team has an Xbox, or a PlayStation. Why don't I take the kids on to *World of Zombies*, put 'em into teams, and show 'em how to play as a UNIT?" He said, "If we are going to start playing video games, we should be playing *FIFA*." I said, "Every kid in the tournament will be playing *FIFA*, so they know all the moves and all the strategies, but what they DON'T know is the world that is *WORLD OF ZOMBIES*!"

 Goofykinggrommet: And yr dad thought playing *WoZ* was a good idea?

Kid Zombie: No. He thought paintballing was a better idea, until I told him paintballing is only for two or three hours, then you have to leave. Play *World of Zombies* and we can do it every day, FOR HOURS AND HOURS, until we get it right. Plus (and this was the match winner), when I showed him how every mission can be kind of like a game of football strategy, and how each DIFFERENT mission could be customised to make DIFFERENT attacking or defending scenarios, he agreed this could be a pretty good way of getting our players to learn TEAM TACTICS, since nobody had learnt anything so far.

So I said, "Make *World of Zombies* COMPULSORY training for the Colts XI, and then every kid in the team will know WHAT TO DO!" So missions like Cat and Mouse, Fireball and Eat the Dog

could become blueprints for how my dad
wants us to line up in the match!!!

 Goofykinggrommet: U got ur dad 2
agree 2 all of that?

 Kid Zombie: Yeah. I mean, he knows it's a
long shot. But it's the only shot we've got.

 Goofykinggrommet: Has he even
PLAYED *World of Zombies*?

 Kid Zombie: Once. But he sucks. I told
him, "U want to get prestiges, you have to
PRACTISE!!" He said he doesn't care about the
prestiges and all that stuff, but he DOES care
that we do OK at the football and he doesn't
look like a COMPLETE idiot in front of Jessica's
mum and her friends, who, BTW, told him how

GREAT it was that he didn't have a REAL job,
so he could spend all his free time chasing
balls with the kids!

So now it's become, like, his MISSION to show
Jessica's mum that the Colts can actually WIN
something.

 Goofykinggrommet: So whaddya
want me to do?

 Kid Zombie: Even I can't play *WoZ* 12
hours a day!!! So I'm gonna introduce some
kids from my team and tell you which
missions I want you to play with them. Then
I'm gonna tell you who needs to be on what
team and what they need to learn.

 Goofykinggrommet: U pull this one
off, Harry, and I will help you on ANY mission

u want. ANY time u want it. When's yr first match?

 Kid Zombie: Saturday. You got six days to get these kids up to speed and hopefully some of 'em will be so pumped they might even start turning up for practice and fitness sessions with my dad. BTW – no pressure, but Bigstock asked me if it was true that I was on a suspended sentence and that, if we did not win the tournament, the board of governors was gonna get rid of me.

 Goofykinggrommet: That's not gonna happen. What did you say?

 Kid Zombie: I told him I didn't know where he got his news from, but us winning the tournament will have ZERO influence on whether I stay at Mount Joseph's.

Goofykinggrommet: Did he believe you?

 Kid Zombie: No. He laughed in my face.

 Goofykinggrommet: Maybe he knows something you don't.

 Kid Zombie: Like what?

 Goofykinggrommet: I don't know. But it wouldn't be the first time he's tried to nail you.

From Harry **to** Charley
01 April 15:04 BST

Dear Cuz –

Here's our fixtures list and route to the FINAL.
Thank God for the floods and the school
holidays! Two of the teams above us in our
group had to pull out, which got us into the
quarter-finals – without even winning a game!
Cool, huh? One team complained that the
competition should be POSTPONED until the
summer term, but the organisers said they
weren't cancelling just because half the West
Country was UNDER WATER!!!

However, the best team in the tournament hasn't
quit, or had a hissy fit, or lost half their players to
family holidays, but they are at the other end of

the draw, so, if we DO get to the final, we'll need something EXTRA special to win, cos these guys win it EVERY SINGLE YEAR. But first we have to beat Sycamore Prep. But you know what? Today we had a FULL turnout for practice at school – which was, like, the first time ever! And after an hour in the gym shouting, *Cat and Mouse! Fireball!* And *Eat the Dog!* my dad said, "Harry? You know something? This might just work!" I said, "I know! How cool is that?"

Anyway, here's the list. I'll let you know how it goes.

Harry

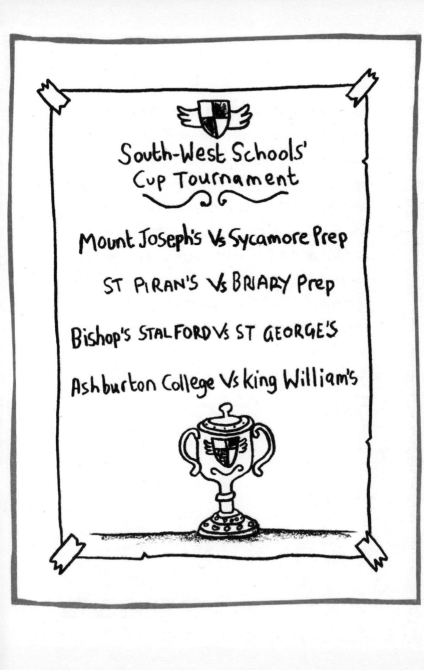

CHAPTER TWENTY-ONE
TOURNAMENT SHOCKER

From Charley **to** Harry
05 April 09:21 PDT

Cuz –

What's goin' on? All I get is radio silence. How
come?

_____

From Harry **to** Charley
06 April 12:21 BST

Dear Cuz –

Check THIS out!! I scanned it for you.

SOUTH-WEST TOURNAMENT SHOCKER!!!

BY SPORTS CORRESPONDENT JOE CARSTAIRS

In an amazing tactical display, tournament underdogs and perennial underachievers Mount Joseph's School **THRASHED** Sycamore Prep 3–1 in the quarter-finals of the South-West Schools' Cup, with goals from Bigstock (2) and Da Silva (1).

When questioned afterwards on how his team had managed to defeat one of the tournament favourites, Coach Wilson Riddles had just one cryptic word in response: Zombies! Son, Harry Riddles, then told this reporter that the use of video games had been instrumental in helping the team achieve this historic victory.

So a most unusual, but clearly effective approach for Mount Joseph's. Well done, Mount Joseph's! We look forward to seeing you in the semis!

And also this...

THE DARTMOOR DART NEWSPAPER, 06 APRIL

MOUNT JOSEPH'S IN ARCTIC BATTLE!!

BY SPORTS CORRESPONDENT JOE CARSTAIRS

In truly atrocious blizzard conditions common only to this bleak part of Bodmin Moor, St Piran's School were narrowly defeated by tournament surprise, Mount Joseph's Prep – even after the game was stopped in the first half to help Cornish farmer Denzel Dannan locate and extract four sheep from a snow drift.

Local Dartmoor boy, Ed Bigstock, son of world famous polar explorer Lord Ned Bigstock, showed his father's natural ability for polar conditions by finding and then digging all the animals out with his bare hands and then going on to score a brilliant hat-trick in almost zero-visibility conditions. A truly remarkable performance from this exceptional young sportsman!

Unbelievably, Mount Joseph's are now one game away from a truly historic and quite extraordinary tournament victory. Well done, Mount Joseph's!

From Charley **to** Harry
06 April 09:15 PDT

Are you kidding me? That's AWESOME! Is
your dad psyched?

From Harry **to** Charley
06 April 17:17 BST

He is, but I think he thinks we got lucky with
the weather against St Piran's and having that
FREAK OF NATURE, Ed Bigstock, on our side.
Dad says he's still got one trump card to play. But
he won't tell me what it is, cos he doesn't know
if he can pull it off!

The bad news is Bigstock got savagely kicked by a
sheep and took knocks to his shin and his mouth,

so now he can't run. Or yell – which, actually, is not a bad thing. But my dad said we'll see how he is on the day.

From Mum **to** Harry
08 April 08:10 BST

Dear sweet boy –

Why don't you write to me any more? What's the matter? Too busy winning? What's going on at home?

Lots and lots of love,

Mummy xxx

From Harry **to** Mum
08 April 08:15 BST

OMG, Mum – you will never guess what just happened! Geoff DUMPED Charlotte when she told him to leave me alone! How about that? I never thought I'd hear my evil sister stick up for me, but she told Geoff he needed to GROW UP and stop making me pull his stupid finger! So he called her some horrible stuff and then she told him to get out of our house, and do us all a favour and move to Australia! So he's gone! YAY!

But you know what I think? I think Spencer might have started texting her and THAT'S why she showed Geoff the door, cos I don't think she would have said a word otherwise. So maybe the Living Dead is gonna be back with the Riddles family again. I hope so. He's much nicer than Geoff. Plus, he never makes me pull his finger.

Harry xxx

From Mum **to** Harry
08 April 08:42 BST

Thank goodness! I never much cared for that boy. But today we have bigger fish to fry. I've asked your sister to video the whole match for me. Good luck!!!

CHAPTER TWENTY-TWO
THE FINAL

From Charley **to** Harry
08 April 12:45 PDT

What happened at the FINAL? GBTM, Smurf!

From Harry **to** Charley
08 April 21:05 BST

What DIDN'T happen, Cuz! OMG, we didn't even GET to the game before it all kicked off on the school bus. My dad gets a call from the hospital saying Mum's having the twins, and he needs to get there FAST, or he's gonna MISS THE BIRTH!!!

So my dad tells the headmaster HE'S going to have to be COACH and TACTICIAN and I can help him and he will get back as soon as he can. Then he gives the headmaster my *World of Zombies* manual and play sheet, which we had copied for every member of the team, and tells Mr Forbes that he'll need to look and learn BEFORE the game starts.

But Mr Forbes is, like, "WHY are we using a *World of Zombies* play manual to coach FOOTBALL?" My dad said he didn't have the time to explain, but trust Harry, cos his system really works!

So basically he left it up to ME to show my headmaster how *World of Zombies* was gonna help Mount Joseph's win the football tournament.

Then Dad jumps in a taxi and tells me he will get back as soon as he can. So now it was, like, just me and the headmaster.

From Charley **to** Harry
08 April 13:08 PDT

And then???

From Harry **to** Charley
08 April 21:30 BST

So we get to the match,
the other team are
waiting to greet us and
every one of these kids
is, like, a FOOT taller
than each one of us. And
leaner. And you can kind
of tell why they ALWAYS
win the cup. They look
like WINNERS!

All of 'em looking super confident. Like they had won the match already. And Bigstock's already complaining about his injuries.

So the game starts and these guys are soon 2–0 up, and all the stuff my dad had drummed into our heads with *Eat the Dog!* and *Burn the Bush!* and all that *WoZ* stuff went RIGHT out the window with the nerves and the fact that most of Mount Joseph's parents had been called up and told to turn out in support of our football team. So there was, like, A LOT of noise. And Bigstock couldn't run properly. Or shout. So we were in BIG trouble.

By the time we got to the end of the first half, they were 3–0 up and it could easily have been 6–0, if it weren't for their centre-forward, who wanted to get the tournament Golden Boot award from his chief rival, Ed Bigstock, so the kid never passed the ball and always took the shot, even when it wasn't on.

Well, then the second half begins and it just goes from BAD to WORSE. They quickly score a goal, nutmegging Bigstock and making this huge mocking celebration of his failed abilities, which turned out to be a GOOD thing, cos Bigstock got so mad he'd been nutmegged that he FORGOT about the pain in his leg and got TWO back before he started limping around again. But this time he was finished and had to be subbed. So now it looked like it was definitely GAME OVER, cos we didn't have any subs.

But then JESSICA and her mum turn up. And that Helmet kid. And Jessica is wearing a Mount Joseph's football strip. So I go over to find out what's going on and I hear her mum tell the headmaster how my dad had called them a few days ago to ask if Jessica would turn out for the team. But her mum hadn't been sure that Jessica could, cos they'd had a holiday booked, but then Helmut arrived, so they'd had to cancel and here they were!!!

Well, the headmaster didn't know what to say, so I told him he had to play her, cos she's awesome. So the headmaster says, "But she's not on the subs list," and Jessica says yes she is, cos my dad told her he would put her on anyway.

So Mr Forbes looks at the team sheet and sees she's down, which he hadn't seen before because he was too busy trying to understand the *WoZ* play manual, and Mr Forbes says, "Great! On you go!" But then their coach comes running over with the ref, saying, "You can't put a GIRL on as a substitute!" And I say, "Why not? She's on the team sheet, she can play!"

Well, their coach looked at Jessica and decided she was not a threat, so he said, "I don't mind if they want to play her. She's only a GIRL!" But the ref still wasn't sure.

And then I suddenly remembered those two movies my dad had given me to watch when he banned me from *WoZ*. So I said to the ref, "Excuse me, sir – are you Scottish?" And the ref tells me he was born in Glasgow. So I ask him if he ever saw a Scottish movie called *Gregory's Girl*. And the ref tells me he LOVES that film. So I say, "What was that story about?" And he says, "It's about this GIRL who plays football for a BOYS school in Scotland." And I say, "Well, there you go then! If she can play football for a tough Scottish school team, why can't Jessica play for us?" So the ref says, "I don't know. That was just a one off." So then I ask him if he's seen a movie called *Bend It Like Beckham*. And the ref laughed and said yes, he liked that film too. I said, "What happened in THAT film?" And the ref said it was about a girl who wanted to play football. So I said, "Well, there you go AGAIN then! She HAS to be allowed to play! Put her on!"

Well, nobody could argue with that, so Jessica comes on and within FIVE MINUTES she has scored TWO GOALS and equalised, cos they didn't mark her properly because they thought she was just, like, some stupid girl!! So we're coming into to the final seconds of the game and they get a break, but they miss and then that's it. The ref blows his whistle for time!

So now it goes to penalties, but Bigstock is done and he can hardly move. So the headmaster says, "Who can take penalties?" Bulmer and Oscar put their hands up and so does Jessica. Then Jessica looks at me and says, "You can do it, Harry! I know you can!" So I put my hand up and now we just need one more and that's it. So the other Tupolev puts his hand up and now we're ready. Kind of.

From Charley **to** Harry
08 April 13:39 PDT

But you guys suck at penalties! You're
English!

From Harry **to** Charley
08 April 21:43 BST

That's where you're WRONG! We had Helmet
and he's GERMAN and they ALWAYS win at
penalties. And even though he couldn't take one,
obviously, because he didn't go to our school,
he asked the headmaster if he could give us
some advice on how to win this, which I thought
was pretty cool of him. So the headmaster said,
"Sure!"

From Charley **to** Harry
08 April 13:48 PDT

Well, what happened??

From Harry **to** Charley
08 April 21:51 BST

Sorry, Cuz – I gotta go to bed now. Night!

From Charley **to** Harry
08 April 13:52 PDT

What the hell, Harry?! You can't do that!!!

From Harry **to** Charley
08 April 22:01 BST

I know. Just KIDDING!!!! So, anyway, we toss a coin, they win the toss and take the first penalty and they score. Then Tupolev takes one and he MISSES. Then they take another one and they score AGAIN!

But now Helmet talks to Bulmer and tells him what to do – and Bulmer shoots and SCORES! So then it's their turn and they are just about to take another one, when Helmet tells Bulmer to start monkeying around and putting the guy off. So Bulmer does a pretty good silverback gorilla impersonation and bingo! Their kid misses. Now it's Jessica's turn. She nails it, no problem. Then they score again. Now we have to score, or we're

328

out. So we do. Then they MISS!!! Now it's all up to ME!! If I score – we win.

So Jessica and Helmet come up to me and tell me to put it low and put it right and I'll definitely score, but I'm REALLY nervous. So then Jessica gives me a peck on the cheek and tells me she knows I can do it cos I never let her down. So now I'm, like, OMG, this is so much pressure!! So I got all this going on in my head.

I run up, but I SLIP as I kick the ball and I think, OMG, I've FAILED! But the ball goes LEFT – not RIGHT, which was where I was told to put it, and where it would definitely have been SAVED! But instead the keeper could only watch and weep as my miss-kicked penalty went left, trickled over the line, then stopped, just the other side of it, winning us the tournament!!!

And that was that! Game, set and match to
Mount Joseph's!!!

After the match, I asked Jessica if she was going
out with Helmet and she said no, cos she wants
to go out with ME!!! So now me and her are

going out. And it's all down to *World of Zombies*! YAY!

_____

From Charley **to** Harry
08 April 14:08 PDT

AWESOME!!! And did you meet yr brothers after?

_____

From Harry **to** Charley
08 April 22:11 BST

Uh-huh. And you know what happened on the way to meet my brothers? I suddenly realised that maybe they SHOULD sleep in MY room, after all, and then we could have bunk beds and we wouldn't need an extension. And I won't need to go to college. Or sleep in the caravan. And my sister won't need to move out of her room (not that she would, anyway). And everything can stay just the way I like it. So then I got to the hospital and saw them, and they were TINY because they were born a bit early, which made me think they should be in my room even more, cos SOMEONE was going to have to keep an eye on them. So I told all this to my mum and she said, "You are SUCH a good kid, Harry. And you guys won the football too? Incredible!" And I said, "Yeah, I know. Now how about that Xbox One?"

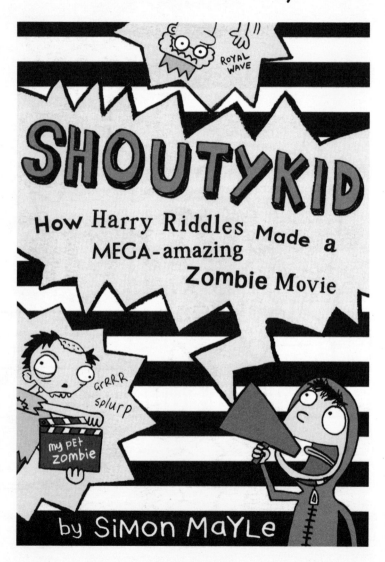

Coming soon: